RODDY M

Body and Soul

Best Wishes & Thanks
to Michael & Margaret
Rustad

Roddy Murray
7·12·13

Acknowledgments

I would like to thank everyone who has encouraged me to complete this book. In particular I would like to thank my brother Sandy for patiently correcting and sub-editing the manuscript. Ewan Cameron, for his time, resources and a roof over my head when I needed it. My mother, Margaret Murray and my children Sebastien, Camille and Elliot for their encouragement. Also a special thanks to Pauline MacGillivray for believing.

Body and Soul

For my parents and for my children.

Body and Soul

Chapter One

Frank Chisholm rounded the final corner of the perimeter running track in his local park at a fierce pace. He was angry, as usual but it gave him strength. Or at least it distracted him from the effort of pushing his 50-year-old body to perform the way it had when he was a young soldier. Anger was useful. This time his anger was directed at his second wife, who had set the bastard lawyers on him again looking for money. Okay, he thought, he hadn't paid her this month or the month before but that was nothing new. He simply didn't have the money right now. He knew she had a part time job, was living with some suit and wouldn't let their son speak to him so why should he pay a penny to her. The bitch!

He had been married three times now. Looking back the marriages all followed a similar pattern. The women had fallen for Big Frank Chisholm the Para with rugged good looks and a body like a boxer which, of course, he was. He had fallen for them and popped the question at some point whilst drunk. Sober he felt obliged to go ahead with the process. After a year or so of physical bliss the women would try to change him to their liking. Specifically, each time they would want him to leave the army. Miffed at his refusal they would fester and eventually leave him while he was away on an operational tour somewhere or on a training course. After a while he managed to stop short of getting married each time but the pattern remained the same.

Twenty-two years in the Parachute Regiment, finishing as a sergeant, then out into the real world. What a shock that had been. All his pension swallowed up by his three ex-wives for his four ex-children and no mates around to keep his spirits up. Three years with seven dead end jobs then two with a succession of bottles as company till he was in shit state. He had always pictured himself going out in a blaze of glory. Outnumbered and outgunned by the enemy but facing them anyway with a gun in his hand. Just like Butch Cassidy and the Sundance Kid. He had never expected to make it to middle age. But he had. No shoot out with overwhelming odds had popped up during his service to strike him down in his prime. If his old Company Sergeant Major hadn't appeared on the scene Frank would have drunk himself to death. Appeared on the scene was an understatement. Paddy Dickman had left the army three years after Frank but had done well for himself. Always the scholar he had acquired all sorts of social work qualifications while serving and was now heading a department that attempted to intervene in time to prevent suicide in men. Flavour of the month in this area of low employment, it was a well-funded department. Paddy needed role models that vulnerable men contemplating ending it all could open up to and get help. Paddy had been Frank's best man at least twice and knew he was the right kind of role model. He also knew that Frank was drinking for Britain and needed help himself.

On the basis of preventing two birds from being killed with one stone he had tracked Frank down to the Bed and Breakfast shithole he was living in. After getting no reply from a loud but civilised knock on the door he had kicked it in. Frank was lying face down on a bed that hadn't been washed or made up properly for months. The room smelled of alcohol, vomit and stale urine. Paddy didn't bat an eyelid. He had seen worse.

After failing to wake Frank he dragged him into the shower which conveniently only produced cold water and turned it on full. The effect wasn't immediate, but slowly the old fighting, kicking Frank began to re-appear, curse the first house guest he had had for six months and try to throw him out. After an initial but futile attempt to punch Paddy's lights out Frank calmed down enough to recognise his visitor.

After being ordered to wash, dress and come out for breakfast they had talked for a long time. As ever they had talked about the old times, the good times and the bad. Old friends, old enemies and how, if they had their time again they wouldn't have changed a thing with the exception of Frank going out shooting in a blaze of glory. Paddy wanted Frank to get back to the Gym, visit various men's clubs giving presentations on spotting the first signs of depression etc. and look for anyone needing help. The aim of Paddy's department was to halve the suicide rate in three years, amongst adult males in the region. It was fully funded for that term and possibly beyond. Frank said it sounded gay, but he realised it was the best and indeed the only offer he had had for a long time. Nobody else would give him a chance in his current state.

He had reluctantly agreed, doubting his ability to kick the booze and face the fresh challenge at the same time. Paddy knew him well enough to share his concern. To avoid any chance of slipping back into his old habits, Frank had been forcibly relocated by Paddy that day to the spare room of Paddy's house. Unlike Frank, Paddy had married once and for life. His wife Mary was one in a million and she had known Frank forever. That didn't necessarily count in his favour but he was an old enough friend of Paddy's for Mary to accept his arrival in her house with good grace.

On pain of death, or at least on pain of pain, Frank had promised not to drink for three whole months and had agreed also that if he did it wouldn't be in Paddy's house.

After asking him to promise, Paddy had stared him in the eye as Frank took the pledge.

"You better commit to this body and soul," he'd said with a genuine hint of menace.

Alone in his bedsit he would have failed but with Paddy, Mary and their kids about he had felt obliged to keep his word. It was very difficult at first. He couldn't remember a time in his life when he didn't drink anything and it took a while to adjust to getting through a day without something to look forward to in the evening.

Paddy had re-established a routine. Frank was re-acquainted with the alarm clock. Not too early at first but slowly going off at an earlier time each day. He went back to having a shower each day, although now a nice warm pleasant power shower. He would walk to the corner shop and buy milk and bread each day as his contribution to the household food bill. Soon he was walking the long way there and back. Then he would take a second walk with the household dog, an ageing spaniel called Para. Para was up for an extra walk initially but as they extended to three then five and eventually ten miles he began to look ill and lose weight. In the end Paddy had to stand Para down and Frank would walk alone. Then he would walk with a rucksack full of clothes. Then one with bricks wrapped in blankets and eventually a rucksack with exercise weights wrapped in blankets.

Also, after a few weeks he would run each day. Not far or fast at first but every day. Unlike most of the people he passed out running, Frank was putting on weight again and felt better for it. His legs began to take on the chunky tree trunk shape they had once had and his upper body was regaining the powerful V-shape which had scared many an opponent in the boxing ring.

Mary increased the quantity of food she cooked accordingly and took pleasure in seeing Frank's recovery. She and Paddy had no secrets and he had given her a no holds barred account of Frank's initial state. Her first concern was for the kids. She didn't want them to witness a drunk staggering about the family home, old friend or not. Paddy had assured her that if he so much as smelled alcohol on Frank's breath he would be history. A promise he relayed to Frank in no uncertain terms. But Frank had been as good as his word and better. As he progressed he started reading bedtime stories to the youngest son, an unplanned but very welcome little boy who was seven; twelve years younger than his sister and fourteen years younger than his brother. Young Daniel accepted Uncle Frank automatically as children do and loved the way he had time to play football with him or build stuff with Lego when his parents did not. Frank even had vague feelings of regret at not spending more time - in fact any time - with his own kids.

Chapter Two

The plant was easy to find. Even for a stranger coming from Glasgow Airport it was easy to find. Take the M77 out of Glasgow till you reach the bypass at Ayr. Go right round the bypass till the end and turn left. Keep going until you are depressed. That's you in Old Cumnock.

The plant itself was the larger of the two new, shiny buildings in the town. The other one being the health centre where most unemployed residents in this ex-mining village go to be treated for respiratory diseases, mental health problems or benefit friendly, non-specific ailments. The factory was much bigger and was purpose built ten years ago to house a workforce of up to 450 with the regularly exercised option of reducing this to just over 200 whenever work was slow. Although many of the major international employers had packed up and left Scotland's silicon glen when the subsidies stopped, Nebus had not. Big names had relocated to new sources of subsidies around the world in the Far East or had moved volume production to the cheap labour pools of newly independent Eastern Europe or China. Nebus had not, for the simple reason that depressed Ayrshire itself had become a low cost manufacturing area and subsidies from panic stricken local authority and Scottish Government agencies had replaced the traditional ones other companies had seen dry up. So their factory in Old

Cumnock had become a rare beacon of employment opportunity in the town and its surrounding area and had also continued to provide high paid employment for some of Scotland's leading engineers in the field of printed circuit board manufacturing. They had migrated to it like large fish trapped in an ever shrinking backwater, often travelling the length or breadth of the country daily in car shares or at the ends of the week to retain their earning levels from better times. Those who couldn't travel daily, or chose not to or couldn't face going home each night to their wives and families lived in a variety of temporary accommodation arrangements in anywhere but Old Cumnock during the week.

To its corporate owners in Omaha, Nebraska it was The Nebus Corporation of America's Old Cumnock Sub-contracting Manufacturing Facility. Ownership confirmed by a well maintained, illuminated sign at the entrance proclaiming 'Nebus Corp'. To everyone who worked or lived there it was simply known as The Corpse.

For senior management in the Corpse the high point for their blood pressure during the calendar year was the annual visit of the Chief Operating officer of Nebus, Blaine McCoard and his European understudy. He would visit every one of Nebus' plants worldwide to brief all the staff personally on the state of the company and its plans for the coming three, 12-month fiscal periods. Or the next three years as Bob, Old Cumnock's boss would translate during his part of the presentation to the few interested souls amongst the large assembled groups. A segment of the presentation which contained only enough American Corporate jargon to confirm his understanding of Blaine's requirements of him and thereafter sufficient plain English to let the Ayrshire workforce know exactly what was going on. Or at least for the ones who cared. Everyone attended the briefings; three per plant where necessary to cover all the shifts, in a total of 13 locations worldwide in regions as culturally diverse as, Malaysia, Eastern Europe, Nebraska, China, Mexico, Thailand and Old Cumnock. Blaine enjoyed these trips for a number of reasons. He was genuinely committed to keeping the workforce of Nebus informed of the exciting plans they had for growth over the next three, 12-month fiscal periods. He felt a personal visit from The Chief Operating Officer of Nebus Corps, to thank them for their recent efforts, showed they were a caring, family-like employer: Values he was keen to promote as an alternative to higher wages. The visits also gave him a chance to meet the real people who turned the corporate vision into a reality day after day and to listen to their thoughts and ideas for the company, the best of which he could steal. But above all else it gave him the opportunity to travel the world for almost two months continuously, sleeping with his stunningly attractive PA Delores

McPhee. Delores' surname was of Irish extraction but the rest of her was a subtle blend of black and Cajun.

All the sources of her ethnicity had sent along of their best and the result was the most beautiful woman who ever visited Old Cumnock. She was tall and slim with perfect dark skin and jet black hair. All the locals agreed she was even prettier than Jean Blackmore who ran the hairdressers. Blaine would have agreed with them wholeheartedly if he had had a clue who Jean Blackmore was. He hadn't exactly stopped loving his wife Beth but had certainly started loving Delores. He enjoyed home life within the narrow confines his timetable allowed. School productions with his children were a particular pleasure, as were the two camping holidays they took each year in the National Parks. He and Beth still made love, but more out of habit than for any other reason. It was, however, not in the same league as six weeks on the road with Delores.

Delores was as enigmatic as she was beautiful. She came from a dirt poor family as far as Blaine was aware but had made it through college on the strength of scholarships and sheer determination. Did she love him, he wondered at times? She never used that word to his face which he found unusual in a woman but put it down to her sense of propriety with him being a married man. Was she simply using him to climb the corporate ladder? Perhaps, he would admit to himself. He regularly mused as to the true motivation for Delores having an affair with him over the past three years. But he always arrived at the same conclusion: He didn't give a monkey's as long as she continued to sleep with him.

The Manufacturing Associates watched the increased tension and apprehension amongst senior managers prior to each visit with a mixture of amusement and resentment. Amusement, because the stresses of the impending visit did not affect them personally one iota. Resentment because they had to clean, tidy and polish every square inch of the plant in the week leading up to the visit in order to create a good (if slightly inaccurate) impression of its normal state. On balance though most of them were happy to watch the stress levels rise amongst the senior management rather than to be paid higher wages at times like this. Many had worked in the plant since leaving school. Some of them through a number of name and ownership changes as Silicon Glen rose and fell. Others had been blown in by the recession from other industries, other local employers or as their own businesses failed. Most were just pleased to have a job if they had families and mortgages to support. For those who had known high pressure jobs in the past this was a time of relief and occasional mild amusement.

Whenever Blaine arrived at a plant for a visit he never failed to be intrigued by the notice boards. Not the showy corporate one's designed to impress the customers. No, they were the same in every plant and he knew them by heart. He had written a lot of the content. It was the staff notice boards he always took the time to read. In particular the staff association notices in each plant. He would find himself reading intimations of forthcoming events like barbecues, concert trips and even paint-balling wondering what it must be like to have the time and opportunity to go on these outings. Being poor, that was what it was like he would remind himself. But still he would find a certain jealousy remaining as he swept on with his world tour, focusing always on the next three, 12-month fiscal periods. Photographs on the noticeboards of people having fun together, smiling and laughing would sometimes haunt him on the longer haul flights when his work was up to date or Delores was asleep. Was he as happy, he would wonder. Did he have any real friends in the same way. Probably not he would conclude. Still, he did have a seven figure salary, share options worth millions and Delores to look forward to so how bad could his life really be? And when all was said and done if you didn't have money you were nothing. Just one of the little people he had spent his life leaving behind.

All in all Blaine loved his job. If not necessarily the day to day nitty gritty of the problems to be solved at least the power and trappings of his position at the top of the corporate ladder. Visiting Scotland and the Old Cumnock plant gave him an enhanced feeling of that enjoyment and certainly his own power. Someone had once joked to him that the Royal Family believe everywhere smelled of fresh paint. For him everywhere he visited in Nebus was freshly cleaned and tidy. A clockwork machine earning millions for its shareholders and more importantly, for Blaine McCoard. He knew it was all done immediately prior to his visits, but then that was part of their purpose. The staff and engineers watched printed circuit boards come off the production lines. For him every one was a little, or sometimes very big bundle of money.

Chapter Three

After three months of recovery Frank felt good. Not just physically but mentally he felt better than he had for a long time. He had surprised himself (as he had Paddy and Mary) at the way he had managed to stop drinking and, somehow, didn't miss it. At this stage Paddy had organised a formal job application for him. After three days of intensive coaching Frank had shown up at the interview in one of Paddy's suits looking the part. An in depth interview chaired by Paddy had resulted in a second and then a formal offer of employment with the local authority as Men's Health Outreach Worker. It still sounded a bit gay to Frank but it was a job. A good job, that he could do. Included in the package was unlimited use of the council's gyms and a car. Frank was on a roll.

The physical recovery had been impressive and with a job requiring him to visit several gyms on a regular basis it could only get better. With Paddy's help he got a nice rented flat near the sea front. With some help from Mary and the kids he got the flat looking really nice. Assisted by dire threats from Paddy he realised he had probably kicked the drinking habit. Life was good.

This job had lasted for five years in total and his sobriety at least as long. The all new Frank Chisholm had even started studying and had gained some qualifications in fitness training and in social work. He ran along the sea front promenade every day whatever the weather and worked out in two different gyms every day. That side of the job had been easy. Gearing up to talking to men's organisations and trying to spot potential suicides had taken longer. As a sergeant in the army he was used to standing in front of groups of men delivering information. The change from shouting at soldiers of The Parachute Regiment and addressing the likes of the local Round Table took some adjustment in the style of his delivery. But not too much he soon realised, as part of the job was to be a macho figure saying that talking about such things was okay and didn't make you any less of a man. He gave out leaflets at the presentations and at the gyms and got talking to lots of interesting guys. Whether by his efforts or by chance the rate of suicide in the region fell steadily enough for the initial three years to be extended to five. After the five years the project was judged such a success by the local politicians that they cancelled the funding and moved on to other hot topics of the day.

Had this happened in the first three years Frank might have struggled to cope with the dispencement of his services. But by the end of five years he had grown strong enough mentally and gathered enough useful qualifications to take it in his stride. That is to say he didn't immediately hit the bottle again. He had also developed a plan to set himself up as a personal trainer to the wealthy, a plan he had discussed at length with Paddy and Mary at their house over Sunday lunch each week. This ritual had started as a means of Paddy checking Frank for any signs of a return to a liquid way of life, but as time went on and Frank clearly wasn't drinking, it became something they all looked forward to.

The idea of becoming a personal trainer had started as a bit of a joke with Frank imagining himself in Hollywood as a personal trainer to the stars. However, it slowly began to take more realistic shape as he learned more about the technical side of physiology, anatomy and the industry itself. He had also started to take a serious interest in nutrition and its part in health and fitness. If you are what you eat then Frank had been a dustbin for about thirty years of his life. A dustbin preserved in alcohol. The all new Frank was quite different though. He had learned about cholesterol, fats, minerals and vitamins. He was now very careful what he put into the finely tuned machine that his body had become. He had attended any formal seminar on the subject which he could and had made a lot of contacts in both the fitness and the scientific communities in Scotland. He had even taken part in a number of studies. He was now in good shape and knew it which made him a useful source of material for some. Similarly almost a lifetime of heavy drinking followed by a late conversion to healthy living made him a gold mine of study material for others. Either way he was fairly confident that his new life would last and survive getting the push from the outreach role.

By the time the five years had finished he already had the qualifications, the contacts and even the business cards to set up as personal trainer to the stars; or at least a few fairly wealthy punters in Ayrshire and Glasgow. After a year he had enough clients to pay the bills. He even ran boot camp training sessions on the seafront near his flat. Not quite P Company he knew, but a profitable little side line.

"I always wondered why more people didn't become soldiers. Looking at you lot, now I know why. You're not up to it. You're weak," he would shout at them as he made them suffer. He would shout and scream at them as though they were recruits. They lapped it up; at £10 an hour each. The more like basic training he made it seem the bigger the classes would become. He even had to get Paddy down to help him out sometimes when he had too many people for one class. Big Frank the Tank was still on a roll.

And so it might have remained if he hadn't had that phone call. It came out of the blue from a research unit on the outskirts of Edinburgh. The boffin who phoned had given his name as Dr Robert Bartleman which had meant nothing to Frank. Bartleman sounded like a Yank, but nobody's perfect, Frank thought to himself. The unit was a commercial venture spun off from one of the universities in Edinburgh and Frank remembered it as one which had carried out some extensive testing of fit people in their middle age some years before. He had taken part at the time and had enjoyed every minute. Total of five hours in the gym each day for a week with scientists who could answer his every question on the human body. An education he would have gladly paid for at the time. Instead he had been paid for his troubles and had been housed at one of the capital's finest hotels throughout. Lovely room, swimming pool and hot and cold running women to talk to every night in the bar. Soft drinks all round of course.

Now they wanted him to come through again, at their expense, for further tests as his profile was "particularly interesting". They would of course pay him and at a more generous rate to compensate for him for having to leave his own business interests and arrange cover. Three weeks in total was on offer. Just him this time apparently, which he reckoned was a big result over the other subjects from the first trial. In a way he was right but not exactly how he imagined at the time. He thought it over for about four seconds before agreeing. They seemed very flexible on exact dates but were keen that it was sooner rather than any later than could be avoided.

Frank started with a call to Paddy to see if he could cover some of the classes. The morning boot camps on the seafront would be easy enough and useful cash into the bargain. The private clients were a non-starter for Paddy though as he was busy with work and committed to being stuck in his office.

"I'm still in touch with a lot of the lads," he told Frank. "Leave it with me and I'll have a ring round"

That evening Paddy phoned Frank back with two names he knew who were reliable and lived in the area. Paddy had seen them recently enough to know they had kept themselves in good shape. Both worked shifts but between them they could cover almost all of Frank's personal training commitments. Hopefully the few clients in the gaps would be understanding enough.

Frank had been busy too. If this trip was anything like the last one he would need to look his best, especially in the hotel bar at night. He had been shopping like a woman he thought; new shoes, new gym kit, new clothes for the evenings and even a new pair of designer pyjamas. He had kept the receipts in the hope that his new fans might pick up the tab. They had sounded so keen for him to come and seemed to have money to burn that you never know. If you don't ask you don't get, he thought. Sometimes you did ask and still didn't get but it was worth a punt.

A new suitcase and a new designer sports bag were included in his new possessions. He wanted to look the part wherever he went with this crowd in the hope that there would be further work from them. He had carefully packed all the new gear in his bags and then gone for a long run in his old running kit. When he had finished the run he stripped off, throwing all of his kit except his training shoes into the bin then had a shower. He dressed in the new tweed jacket he had treated himself to, matched with a very expensive pair of designer jeans and waited for the courtesy car which Nebus Bioscience had kindly insisted on sending for him. He had visions of a stretched limo with a big black driver come minder from New York in livery wearing a matching peaked cap but anything smart and free would do.

In the event, five minutes before the appointed time, a large Audi estate pulled up from one of the local agencies that serviced Prestwick Airport with a local guy in a well-worn suit. Only slightly disappointed, Frank grabbed his bags and placed them carefully in the boot of the car.

"I'm Frank," said Frank to the driver of the Audi.

"Bob," the driver replied shaking hands and wondering vaguely why someone would pay the agency rates to drive Frank to the outskirts of Edinburgh. But really he didn't care. Frank was chatty and pleasant enough, unlike some of the passengers he'd had to drive over the years. The whys and wherefores didn't matter.

Chapter Four

This year's visit was going particularly well, Blaine thought to himself. As the plants in the U.S. struggled to even maintain volume, Scotland was benefitting hugely from European demand. Old Cumnock was close to its capacity workforce of 450 and he and his European manager had already discussed a second Scottish plant in serious terms. All they needed now was a sufficiently frightened local authority to pay for it all, and they had one in mind on the other side of the country. Money was being made here which more than made up for the drop in profits in the States and that meant that Blaine could stay bullish about the whole company in his quarterly results briefings when the CEOs of other similar companies could not. This made him popular with shareholders, staff, business journalists and the banks. All the faces in front of him, for all their poor grooming and apathy, had brought him success whether they liked it or not. He certainly liked it. He genuinely hoped that they were pleased with his lavish praise and promises of job security for the foreseeable future.

Delores had excused herself from this particular presentation for two good reasons. Firstly, she was reading a good book and wanted to finish it. Secondly, it was to the night shift of Old Cumnock and was taking place late at night. As a result she had stayed at the hotel and taken advantage of its wide variety of health treatments and its visiting hairdresser, a pretty, local girl called Jean Blackmore who had taken great interest in Delores' hair. Thus pampered and groomed to perfection she was sitting in the lobby of the hotel reading her book. She knew Blaine would be some time yet but hopefully by the time he had briefed the nightshift her book would be finished and she could focus on making his dreams come true in the hotel room. That was what he wanted and that was what he would get. Partly because he was fun and worked very hard at pleasing her in bed. Partly too, because this had given her career a boost when others had struggled. Most of all, though, because when she was with Blaine she felt safer and further away than she had ever felt before from the grinding poverty she had grown up with.

Although the book was absorbing she couldn't help looking up each time somebody walked into the hotel. People-watching was almost as much fun as a good book. Where were these people from? Was that man with his wife or his secretary? Was she really going out with him? No doubt some people-watchers asked the same questions about Delores and Blaine. At 50, he was 20 years older than she was. He had put on a few pounds more than suited him. Quite a few pounds. He was quite tall but neither dark or handsome. But what was clear as soon as you looked at him was that he was confident, rich and successful. That would be reason enough the watchers would think, for a girl like Delores to go out with him.

As the automatic doors whirred open near midnight, Delores looked up and almost dropped her book. Through the door strode the Chairman of Nebus, Dan Bartleman.

Dan was a billionaire several times over and the largest shareholder in Nebus. He was the largest shareholder in a number of companies but took a particular interest in Nebus as he saw it as the best bet for stellar growth at this time. He was in his early 70s but had the drive and determination of a man half his age. And one who had better knees. He limped as he walked but he still walked quicker than most people. As a result he had left his travelling companion some distance behind. Dan turned and shouted "come on man" to an unseen figure in that unique way of his which was at the same time both jovial and career threatening.

After a pause long enough for the automatic doors to close and then open his companion caught up. Delores was again taken by surprise. The trailing figure was the corporate doctor, Victor Zelnik who, as far as she was aware, had never left Nebraska before on company business. He may never have left Nebraska full stop.

She had a moments panic in case Dan was annoyed at her missing the nightshift's presentation but she needn't have worried.

As soon as he saw her he limped over at speed and said, "Good evening Delores. I am so please to find you here alone. Vic and I have taken the jet over to see Blaine on a matter of supreme urgency. Having you here will cushion the blow."

Delores was reeling at this and asked what was wrong. A dozen different possibilities swirled round her head, most of which involved Blaine getting fired.

Unfortunately, Dan had said all he was going to say on the subject for now.

"Can't say any more till Blaine gets here. He has to hear it first," he said.

Delores knew better than to press for details but was worried sick, as much for her own future as for Blaine's.

Dan moved to the reception as his luggage was brought in from the car. A single suitcase which she recognised as the emergency one he kept with the corporate jet. No luggage arrived for Dr Zelnik. This was even more worrying, suggesting as it did that he had been dragged away from his routine of annual health checks in such haste that he had not been given time to pack. This was confirmed as she heard Zelnik organise a toothbrush, paste and other basics from the receptionist.

Dan ordered a waiter, so that he could order a drink and joined Delores while he waited. They sat in silence which was unusual for Dan. When the waiter arrived he asked for a double scotch to which the waiter reeled off a long list of available options. Dan looked up bemused and impressed at the same time before remembering that he was, after all, in Scotland. After a pause he ordered a Macallan which was in truth the only one of the list he could remember. He looked at Delores to suggest she also ordered a drink. She rarely did but decided that in the circumstances a gin and tonic might be wise. When Zelnik, a lifetime teetotaller, ordered a large bourbon she knew there was trouble ahead.

Before and after the drinks arrived Dan forced them all into making small talk about the company, his flight over, the Scotch, in fact anything that came into his head. In this way they passed the time till Blaine arrived back from briefing the Old Cumnock staff.

When he did arrive at the hotel, greatly anticipating a beautiful and fragrant Delores waiting alone for him in the lobby, he was rather annoyed to see her sitting with two older men. When he realised who they were though, he immediately cancelled any anticipation of a night in the sack with Delores and put on his best poker face. The one he wore to emergency meetings when they occurred. The face that said to everyone: "Whatever it is, Blaine McCoard can deal with it, so don't worry." He wasn't sure this time if it was working.

Dan Bartleman rose to his feet when he saw Blaine and limped a swift three paces to shake his hand.

"How'd it go son?" he asked.

"Good thanks. I think job security is the biggest issue here and I was able to give them that in spades," said Blaine. He noted Dan's head nodding and also noted that Dan didn't give a shit about his answer. This was not good but Blaine couldn't think why on earth Dan was here or why old Zelnik had tagged along. Maybe Dan was ill. He saw Dr Zelnik sneak a sip of Bourbon and thought: "Christ! Dan must be very ill."

Dan didn't sit down but gestured that Blaine should. He paused without speaking for a second or two and did some strange hand rubbing thing that none of them had seen him do before. Usually he got straight to the point; went straight for the jugular if necessary. But not tonight.

"Blaine, Vic and I have flown in with some news for you. Not good news I'm afraid," said Bartleman. "I've asked Vic to give you the low down then we'll talk together in private."

With that he indicated without room for doubt that Delores should follow him as he limped at speed to the residents lounge. She followed looking back at Blaine with a shrug of the shoulders which told him she was no wiser to events than he was. Blaine was starting to worry. Things had a pattern in Nebus under Dan Bartleman.

Everyone in senior management knew where they stood, especially if it was on thin ice. 'Dan the man' did not shy away from delivering bad news, whether it was to shareholders or board members. If he was here to fire Blaine, and he could think of no good reason why he would, he would have delivered the salvo himself. He would never deputise that one and certainly not to old Doc Zelnik who had nothing to do with business operations.

"Nice place here," mumbled Zelnik and then started again. "Blaine I'm here with the results from the last annual medicals. You know we do every possible test we can on the senior staff. I like to think it's because we work for a caring employer but we both know it is so that any threat to the bottom line from senior staff's ill health is picked up as early as possible. We can then hopefully treat them successfully or minimise the impact of their illness with succession planning before things go public."

Blaine was hearing Vic Zelnik talk but the words were from Dan Bartleman's vocabulary. What on earth was this about? Was Dan about to snuff it and wanted Blaine ready to step in. Dan could be a terrifying person to deal with but Blaine felt they had always got on well. He liked Dan's no nonsense approach to business and, if he was in fact ill, Blaine would genuinely miss the old bastard.

Zelnik's next words hit him like a rifle shot.

"I'm afraid you are very ill, Blaine. There's no easy way to break this but you are terminally ill with cancer."

Blaine sat back, wounded. He stared at Zelnik hoping he had mixed up the words and said the wrong thing but the unusually steely professional look staring back at him said no. He had always found Dr Zelnik, or Old Vic as he was affectionately known, a figure of amusement at Nebus. Unconcerned by profit margins or quarterly figures, he seemed to bimble about his medical suite taking samples and dispensing painkillers or other basic pills to the staff at head office almost as a bit of comic relief to the serious matter of making money which engrossed everyone else there. Now he was not a figure of fun, there was no amusement from the calm, bedside manner he used to describe Blaine's impending death.

Blaine started floating and swaying as Zelnik detailed the test results, the double checks which had been carried out and the confirmation of secondary cancers. He had once watched a film set at the outbreak of WW2. In it some poor general had had to tell President Roosevelt about Pearl Harbour. He felt dizzy and sick as Zelnik told him how bad his own Pearl Harbour was.

"How long have I got?" Blaine finally managed to ask.

"A maximum of six months," said Zelnik after a pause.

Six fucking months, thought Blaine. Six months at best by the sound of it. That meant he might just last for one final Christmas with his wife and kids but there was no chance of another six week tour with Delores. He only vaguely felt guilty at wishing it was the other way round.

"There must be something I can do to stop it or slow it down. Christ, hasn't medicine come up with a cure for this yet," Blaine almost shouted.

He was angry and was taking it out on Zelnik. He knew this was wrong and knew also that he had been ignoring the symptoms and pains he'd been getting for months before the annual check-up. It was partly that normal male, macho shit that denies any problems with one's health automatically. But he had to admit that he had not wanted anything to get in the way of his grand tour with his gorgeous PA.

After a few minutes which had seemed to last a lifetime Dan Bartleman re-joined them without Delores. In what seemed a pre-arranged move, Dan nodded to Zelnik who got up and walked towards the bar with obvious relief spreading over his face and indeed his movements.

Dan took the vacated chair and looked long and hard at Blaine to gauge his state of mind. It was not just that Blaine had made him a whole heap of money and had the potential to make a whole heap more which went through his mind. Although a man of ruthless business tendencies, Dan had grown to like Blaine and regard him as the nearest thing to a friend amongst the senior staff of the companies he controlled. This news would devastate everyone who had to face it but if anyone could deal with it and stay focussed it would be Blaine McCoard. Dan needed to know that Blaine was still capable of listening, reasoning and considering options before he started his next pitch.

"How you doing son," he asked with genuine concern.

"Oh, reeling a bit from Old Vic's news I'm afraid but hanging in there, I guess."

Dan looked hard into the younger man's face and decided the mental toughness needed to run one of his global companies appeared to have survived the bombshell.

"I can't tell you how sorry I was to hear the news. Vic came to me with it first to ask my advice on how to break it to you. I hope you don't mind son."

Blaine knew that any news which might affect any aspect of Nebus's performance or share price would go to Dan first. He suspected he would hear about the second coming before anyone else did if it ever happened and would have share options ready to take full advantage.

"Of course not," he replied in a stronger voice than he had expected. "I appreciate you coming over with him. I know how busy you are."

Dan took comfort from the tone of resolve in Blaine's voice and pushed on.

"Vic has confirmed that conventional medicine holds no hope for curing you at this point in time," he said deliberately not sugar coating the truth. "I want you to know that whatever happens we will provide and pay for any treatment needed to ease things and Beth and the kids will be taken care of whatever. However, I want to discuss an option that may be of interest to you which Zelnik knows nothing about."

Dan looked around the lobby carefully to ensure that nobody was within earshot.

"As you know the Nebus parent company has a diverse range of interests throughout the world ranging from defence to medical and some charitable foundations. All of which are profitable. Within the medical portfolio we have a subsidiary called Nebus Bioscience."

Blaine looked at Dan wondering what the fuck he was talking about. He had mentioned options, which were non-existent as far as Old Vic was concerned, but he now appeared to be giving Blaine a briefing on Nebus Holdings Inc. which he certainly could do without at this exact moment in time thank you very much. The old guy is losing it he thought to himself with an edge of bitterness and self-pity which he was not used to and didn't much like.

Dan continued unconcerned by Blaine's expression.

"Nebus Bioscience was set up to tap into the possibilities of cloning and any marketable spin-offs. Remember Dolly the sheep?"

Blaine nodded, vaguely remembering the news story and wondering if Nebus saw sheep as a profitable side-line.

"Various strands of research developed from that within Nebus, looking at everything from life extension to hair restoration, both of which are potentially hugely profitable markets. A lot of work was done on the separate brain development of some of Dolly's clones, exploring the way brain pattern affected the life expectancy of each sheep. In the end that avenue proved to be a heap of shit and was cancelled but the brain pattern research continued with a lot of success and was viewed as having potential for other applications. Now, my nephew Robert heads up the main unit near Edinburgh and reports to me personally. Recently his researchers had a breakthrough in mapping the human brain and personality traits using some of the superfast computers our military division has developed. These computers are so powerful that for the first time they have the capacity to record and store the entire brain function of a human brain."

Blaine was listening politely or he hoped his face suggested as much but he was still more concerned with dying, telling his wife and kids the good news and having a relatively short time left in sufficient good health to appeal to Delores. Identical sheep and Dan's nephew's brain weren't even in the Top 100 things he gave a shit about at this time. But for whatever reason this was all important to Dan and so he kept listening with part of his own brain.

"Recently," Dan continued, "Robert's team successfully recorded the full mapping of a rat's brain on their computer. They were then able to replicate it in the brain of another rat. Test's on the second rat proved that it behaved exactly like its donor rat and remembered lessons it had learned regarding feeding apparatus, etc."

Dan paused to make sure Blaine was still with him. A nod suggested he was.

"Now this is where you come in."

Blaine started to give Dan his full attention again.

"Robert is convinced that a full transfer of all brain function took place, including a full copy of the rat's memory and if so there was no reason why this could not be replicated with a human being."

Blaine looked at Dan trying to understand exactly what he was saying but could not fully get it.

Dan saw his difficulty and went on, "In other words we think we can map the full extent of a human brain and transfer it to another one. To put it bluntly we could record everything that you are, what you know, can do, everything you remember and transfer it from your present body to another healthy one."

Dan stopped to see if the implication of this had sunk into Blaine's delicate consciousness.

"Are you kidding," said Blaine without the customary respectful tone he always had for Dan. "I'm going to die soon and you're trying to give me hope with some hair brained (no pun intended) scheme to transfer me to somebody else's body. It may have seemed to work with a rat or two but a human is different. I don't want to be the guinea pig for your first go on a human. If I only have a few months left then so be it, but I'll live it to the full while I can without being lobotomised by your nephew."

Then after a pause with some element of respect, "Thank you for your concern, though."

Again Dan looked round to check that nobody else could hear him then continued.

"You would not be the first guinea pig. Our partners in the military provided two suitable trial subjects for us. Terrorists or something like that. Not Americans anyway. Robert's team flew to the States and spent three weeks mapping the brain patterns and functions of both. Once they were sure they had recorded it all accurately they successfully stopped the brain functions of both and then re-started both brains with each other's maps. The experiment was successful."

Blaine was reeling for the second time today. "So these people woke up in the wrong bodies and just accepted it."

"Not quite. The first couple of trials weren't as successful. The subjects had huge compatibility problems and failed to adjust to the new setting but Bobby worked that out too. Both subjects have to have a certain amount in common such as approximate age, height, blood type and most important of all their brain maps have to be broadly similar in a number of ways. For example a driven, go getter needs to be put into a similar host. I'm not a boffin I'm a money man as you know but Bobby has it pretty well sussed. He has a medical degree and a PhD in something really technical to do with computing. I paid the bills so I should know but he also has an MBA from Harvard to make sure it all made money. That was a condition of mine for funding the other studies. Bottom line is he says it's safe and knows what he is talking about. So what do you say?"

Blaine was up to speed or beyond in anything to do with semi-conductor manufacturing but this sounded way beyond what was possible. Even if Dan and his nephew could now do this he had serious concerns. Dan hadn't mentioned the unsuccessful trials to start with for one. For another who was going to volunteer to swap bodies with a terminally ill, overweight executive. Then there was the question of how he would explain his change of appearance to Delores and all his friends. And, Christ! His wife and kids. No this was madness from start to finish and he was about to say so when he changed his mind. It surprised him how calmly he could reason about this. But then that had been the way with many previous conversations with Dan. Calmly discussing the options and ways out of a crisis situation while suppressing the sheer terror he should have felt. Why should this be any different he thought.

"Okay Dan. Suppose this is possible, and I am really suspending disbelief here. Why would anyone swap with me?"

He had decided to go through the main questions which had arisen in his head, one by one and this seemed the best one to start with.

"Money probably or someone facing death in prison, we're working on that right now back at head office. Bobby is also up all night on this going through all his files and previous assessments to come up with a suitable candidate. My gut feeling is that it won't be too difficult to get a match."

Blaine continued with question after question and found Dan ready with a confident reply to each. After a while he slumped back in his chair exhausted. Dan could see it in Blaine's face. Not just the fatigue from work, travel and the bad news tonight but for the first time he realised that Blaine looked ill.

"Listen son, you've had quite an evening of it tonight and need some rest. Your commitments tomorrow will be cancelled by my assistant when the plant opens in the morning. Get some sleep and have a long lie if you can manage it but remember this. We need you to run this company and move on to bigger things within the parent group and we are prepared to do whatever it takes to keep you if we can. But above all else remember that, ill as you are, you don't have to die."

Dan stood up and in a reversal of the norm which both men thought nothing of, he helped Blaine to his feet. They made their way slowly to the bar where Vic Zelnik was back to drinking his customary fruit juice and Delores was nowhere to be seen.

The doctor explained that he had told Delores merely that Blaine wasn't 100% and would need some time off for treatment and to recuperate. She was probably smart enough to realise Dan Battleman didn't usually fly round the world helping deliver such news and there must be more to it. Either way she was definitely smart enough to politely express her concern and head off to her room alone to maintain a sense of propriety with Dan here. Blaine would tell her soon enough. Probably tomorrow to avoid any chance of being caught together in the same hotel room.

Blaine refused another drink and said good night to Dan and Zelnik. But he did accept a sleeping pill from the doctor before heading to his room; 7.5 mg Zopiclone; very much the entry level for insomniacs. Without it he knew there was little chance of sleeping and boy did he need to sleep. Jet lag, energetic nights with Delores on top of the normal cares and strains of running a multinational would have exhausted even a well man. Blaine now knew for definite that was one thing he was not.

Chapter Five

On the journey Frank had started to ask Bob about Nebus Bioscience in the hope he had some inside gen but Bob had never heard of them before and couldn't help. So instead they had passed the journey talking about football, music, politics and anything else that came to mind. Bob had asked if Frank was flying out somewhere as the booking was to take him to the Hilton beside Edinburgh Airport and that seemed logical. Frank had wondered about making up some exotic destination but in the end had just said enigmatically he had to meet some people there.

This had set Bob's mind off on a range of possibilities. Frank didn't look or sound like a chief executive, corporate lawyer or even a sales rep. Sneaking a look over at Frank at that point in the conversation he had decided hit man was more likely. An anonymous meeting, an exchange of envelopes over lunch at the Hilton then Frank would fly out to somewhere in Africa or the Middle East, pop the mark then fly back, collect a second envelope and vanish without a trace. Bob read too many thrillers.

Eventually they reached the Hilton and declining Bob's offer of help, Frank grabbed his bags and walked into the

Hotel. He walked up to the reception where a very attractive Polish girl asked if she could help.

"The name's Chisholm," said Frank. "There should be a reservation for me."

Frank loved this.

"Yes Mr Chisholm," confirmed the receptionist. "We have you booked in for three weeks through Nebus."

She handed him the keycard for the room and asked him to sign the form she printed out with his check- in details on it. Declining her offer of help with his luggage (he assumed she would organise some pimply youth to help rather than accompanying him to the room herself) he picked up his two bags, flexing all his muscles which were visible to the receptionist and walked to the lift. Looking back the receptionist had returned to her paperwork unimpressed. Not to worry, thought Frank, three weeks of residency in which to pull gave him plenty of time.

The lift went up one floor and the door pinged open. Frank made his way to his room and opened the door. The room was large and made a mockery of the average barrack room he'd had to stay in during his years in the Paras. He was pleased to note that his was a 'delux room plus', suggesting the good people at Nebus Bioscience were intent on rather spoiling him. A large 32 inch TV screen and a very comfortable easy chair to sit in whilst watching it caught his eye, although he suspected the large desk and office chair would remain unused during his visit. The bed looked suitable for all purposes he might need it for, even a good night's sleep. It also faced the TV screen on the opposite wall so the comfy chair would see less use too. He wondered if the in-house entertainment included porn and if Nebus would pay for that, then decided not to push his luck.

The arrangements had been to settle in that day and be ready for a courtesy vehicle at nine the next morning. He had arrived with enough time to use the swimming pool and gym before making the most of the restaurant which was called The Space, combining bar, restaurant and lounge. It promised a menu with foods geared towards productivity and natural energy boosts. He suspected Nebus would put that to the test but he was ready for anything they could throw at him. All this luxury and a fat cheque at the end of it. Frank was lapping it up.

His plans for the evening went better than he could have hoped for. A fairly easy hour or so in the gym, upping the tempo just enough to impress whenever any female entered, was followed by a few lengths in the pool. While he was in the gym a classy lady of about 40 or so had come in and done an energetic 25 minutes on the cross trainer. Frank had been sure at the time she was eying him up but had tried to stay aloof. As he left for the pool, however, he had nonchalantly smiled as he passed her and said good evening. She had later followed his lead to the pool and swam several lengths herself. He had finished his visit to the leisure complex with a visit to the sauna and knew he had scored when the lady joined him there.

Her name was Charlotte from Carshalton, which she explained was part of the London borough of Sutton. Frank nodded his head as if fascinated but really didn't give a monkey's where she came from. She obviously worked out on a very regular basis, having a slim figure that belied her years. She was a project manager with one of the big banks and was here to train a group of staff in their Edinburgh headquarters on a new reporting system. Normally she would have been put up in a budget hotel in the city centre but everywhere had been full for the dates she was there so she got lucky and ended up at the Hilton. Four days down and three to go she was enjoying her first visit to Edinburgh although she admitted she had been quite lonely so far, being well out from the town centre.

Your lonely nights are over thought Frank as he asked if she fancied joining him for dinner as he too was here alone. Her speed at accepting confirmed Frank's assessment of the situation. He would not be needing the in-house porn tonight. As she stood up to leave she squeezed his thigh for support and he knew he was in.

After a shower in his room and getting dressed in some of his coolest new clothes Frank headed for The Space and a night with Charlotte from Carshalton. She was already there before the appointed hour wearing a sprayed on dress which showed off her figure to its best advantage. A plunging neckline kept his attention most of the meal and he sincerely hoped that the food did indeed give you energy and improve your performance or whatever they had promised.

She was initially surprised that he didn't drink but his job as a professional trainer explained that to her satisfaction. It avoided any discussion of his previous drinking patterns and she decided from his fitness level and build that he must always have looked after himself and said so. Little did she know, thought Frank, but this was no time to be uneconomical with the truth.

She seemed very impressed with his tales of army life and tours of Northern Ireland and Bosnia. He'd been in the first Gulf War and Gulf 2 'The Sequel' as he called it. She laughed at that and moved her hand to hold his. They finished their desserts quickly after that, declined the offer of coffee from the waiter and headed for Frank's room at a trot.

Chapter Six

The next day Blaine slept deep and slept late. Instead of getting up at his customary six o'clock he didn't even wake till nine and then he was groggy and dosed over again till almost ten o'clock. When he did get up he was still a bit hazy from the Zopiclone but he felt rested. It took a minute or two to remember the conversations of the night before and when he did for a moment or two he wondered if they had all been a dream. But slowly he came round to realising that he was in fact dying and Dan was in fact mad. Or more accurately had proposed a mad scheme to him which sounded unlikely to solve problem number one.

After a shower and a coffee made with the room's instant beverages kit, he dressed and went down to breakfast around half ten. Officially breakfast finished at ten but normal rules did not apply to Dan Bartleman so Blaine was not surprised to see Dan and Delores waiting for him at a table in the dining room with a waiter standing by to take any food orders, whatever time they might come. Blaine said good morning to them both and ordered his usual full English.

When the waiter had gone to pass the order to a no-doubt furious chef, Blaine looked at the other two to gauge the mood of the house. Dan was Dan and was looking back at Blaine to assess his mental state and to see if he had reached a decision. Delores looked as if she could have used one of Old Vic's Zopiclone's but was as beautiful as ever, if slightly dark around the eyes from lack of sleep.

Truth be told, Blaine had been thinking as he showered and dressed. If he treated the situation as he would a problem with the business, without any emotion, then it was really quite straight forward. The choice was simple. Live for a few months in rapidly failing health and then die, leaving behind a wife and kids and never seeing Delores again being the first, rather stark option. The alternative was to go ahead with Dan and young Bobby 'the boffin' Bartleman's hair brained scheme and die much sooner or if they were right and he was the mad one, survive in good health as if nothing had happened, albeit in someone else's body.

The second option certainly sounded the brighter of the two. Even if he didn't make it and his brain fried in one of Bobby's super-computers he would at least avoid a lingering death. The chance of surviving did appeal to him though. He was essentially a fairly moral individual outside of the boardroom and he had issues to clarify regarding the 'donor' but these, as Dan had said, were details to be worked out.

He looked at Delores who was trying hard to look like a merely concerned PA whose boss was unwell rather than a worried girlfriend whose lover was very unwell. She looked back with a look of concern but a questioning look too, which confirmed that Dan had still kept her out of the full loop.

They made small talk till Blaine's breakfast arrived at which point Dan said he had calls to make and would like to speak to Blaine in his room at midday. Blaine recognised this as a meeting where a decision had to be made. Doesn't give folk much time to adjust he thought to himself before turning to Delores.

"What has Dan told you so far," he asked in a gentle voice.

"He says you're very ill and need treatment then rest. He says you can make a complete recovery but it all depends how you approach it. I don't really understand. I could hardly ask him any more without giving the game away. You know his attitude to office affairs."

Blaine did. He knew he would be safe enough while he was making Dan lots of money but Delores would be seen as a potential distraction to the process and would be toast.

"Dr Zelnik thinks I'm dying of cancer. Dan thinks his nephew Bobby can maybe save me with some radical new treatment." It was a very abridged version but Blaine didn't want to go into any more details at the moment. Not until he had a chance to speak to Dan again.

Delores asked lots of questions about the cancer and he told her pretty much all he knew. Fortunately she didn't ask much about the treatment. He'd mentioned after the first question about it that he didn't really understand any details but that Dan had already spoken to his nephew who was on the case. They talked about other shared things for a time after that. Blaine loved the way she accepted whatever he could spare of himself and his time during the busy daily or annual schedule. He was even more convinced that he loved her and almost promised himself, though not her yet, that if he beat this one he would leave Beth and spend the rest of his life with her.

Delores looked round to see if anyone was watching them but there was no one to be seen and she suddenly rose to her feet and kissed him quickly but firmly on the lips. He smiled at her with a rare gentleness in his face and knew he would do whatever he had to if there was a chance of more time with her. If he had been in any doubt about it before he was in no doubt now. If Dan and Bobby had a way of saving him in any shape or form then he would take it. If it didn't work then he would peg out early but still looking healthy enough to be remembered fondly by all concerned. Especially Delores.

They sat in silence for a while with nothing else really to say. Eventually it was time to head off to Dan's room and sort out a plan of campaign. Blaine kissed Delores as he left without even looking round to see if anyone was watching. He was past caring about such trivia. She smiled and briefly held his hand, letting it trail out of hers as he turned and walked off to the elevator.

Dan was in the biggest room available in the hotel. It was still small by US standards but it was a roomy enough suite compared to Blaine's room. Dan was sitting in front of his lap-top and was on the phone as well, apparently doing two things at the same time. He looked up and smiled at Blaine as he entered and motioned him to sit on one of the comfortable chairs ranged round the table. Blaine sat down suddenly weary despite his solid night's sleep. For the first time he realised that he was ill and it was affecting his energy levels. He must have been fighting it and working through the fatigue for weeks if not months. Now that he knew the worst he seemed to lack the resolve to fight it in the same way. Maybe it was just the after effects of the sleeping pill but he suspected it was more than that.

After a long conversation on the phone, Dan turned and faced Blaine with his full attention. Again he was looking to gauge how the younger man was holding up and to look for the resolve that had made him so successful as head of Nebus. He seemed confident there was enough of it to continue without further ado.

"Let's talk turkey," Dan began. "You are the most successful CEO within the Nebus Holdings group and you make the shareholders a lot of money. Our contingency planning around senior figures would regard your loss to the company as a force majeure. We are prepared, therefore to do whatever we can to prevent that happening, whatever that requires. In the circumstances the options are very narrow. We are looking at bringing forward the next stage of testing on our brain mapping programme to include you and therefore give you, what Bobby and I believe to be, a good chance of a full life."

He moved forward in his chair and in a softer tone added, "I also regard you as a friend and want to help you as such in any way I can. Have you had a chance to consider the options?"

Blaine nodded and took a deep breath. A process which he noticed now hurt a little bit in his guts. "I am sceptical of this process Robert's been working on but it looks like I have no other option. I need to understand the details a bit better and don't understand what happens if it does work. How would my wife and family react? How on earth could you find a donor willing to swap places? My body is not exactly highly desirable real estate. I am in this job by paying attention to the details and these things don't square as far as I can see. Help me here Dan."

Dan nodded, pleased to see that Blaine was dealing with his current difficulties in broadly similar terms to a business problem. That suggested he was dealing with it better than most would have.

"Okay son, I appreciate what you're saying and as ever let's take it one thing at a time and work through the problem. I spoke to Bobby earlier and he has been combing through personal records on our data base and the data bases of our associates including the military and other agencies I am not at liberty to name. I spoke to him this morning and he has found as close to a perfect match as we could hope for from a research project that was carried out here in England some years back. There were four possibles worldwide but this guy looks a lot like you too and has money problems from three ex-wives and countless children. He's some kind of veteran, airborne or similar who believes he can beat the cancer with a special diet he has developed. I hope he's right but either way he will sign up for $2 million. One for him and one to square things with his cast-offs. Good news for you is he is as fit as a fiddle and has no health problems whatsoever. Bobby phoned him this morning and is waiting for dates but we have told him not to hang around."

Blaine stared at Dan looking for any down side but there was none. He couldn't believe how easy that sounded but then the world was full of strange people and many of them had money problems. He nodded and waited for Dan to continue.

"As for the problem with your wife, I want you to think long and hard about this one. It has not escaped my notice that you and Delores are more than just colleagues." He put up his hand to make sure Blaine didn't try any pointless denial which might later prove embarrassing to them both. Blaine saved his breath and just nodded. After all they were talking turkey here and time was precious to him now, whatever lay ahead.

Dan went on without pulling punches. "This may be an opportunity to tidy things up a bit. Anyone facing what you're facing would reassess his life at this moment. What was important to him? His children certainly. His wife? Well perhaps for some, but Delores is a little bit out of the ordinary. Wouldn't it be nice to have an opportunity to come clean and be honest with all concerned? You hardly see Beth these days or your kids. If you saw your kids the same amount of time or more and went home to Delores every day without having to go half way round the world to do it; wouldn't that be a welcome outcome?"

Blaine didn't agree but similarly he didn't disagree with what Dan was proposing. Dan took his silence as a cue to continue.

"From the point of view of accepting the "New you", it will be far easier if you're with Delores. After all, she is a company gal and could be in on the whole deal from the outset. Even if she wanted to tell anyone we have her by the short and curlies legally. She tries to blab and we can use the courts to keep her quiet. Not that she would of course. Think long and hard about it Blaine."

Blaine was reeling a bit inside again but there was, within the dizziness, the outline of a firm plan taking shape. If he did nothing he was dead and it wouldn't really matter who he had wanted to be with. If Bobby could pull this off he would have a lifetime to spend with one woman or the other. Dan hadn't said it but Blaine knew if he tried to continue seeing both his wife and Delores afterwards action would be taken. Dan didn't like conflict endangering the productivity of his top people and he would show Delores the door. Facing the reality of his health problems was the perfect time for a clean break, a fresh start. Beth might even be more sympathetic in the circumstances. He wasn't quite so sure on that one though, she could be pretty determined when her dander was up. Hell hath no fury and all that. Still the main issue at this point was whether to risk the procedure or not. It sounded too fantastic to be true but Dan wasn't the joking kind and seemed convinced.

"This airborne guy is definitely okay going along with it? Even that sum of money is little compensation for volunteering to have terminal cancer. I thought everyone in Britain got looked after by the state whether their ex contributed or not. Why the cash for his ex's."

Dan looked at him without blinking. "It is a lot of money. We'll do it in a way his ex-wives are all off his back for good. Our English legal department are working on it now. We wouldn't have had to pay as much in the States where poor people are also scared people without health care. But we only had four possibles and I didn't think you would fancy waking up Black or Hispanic."

Blaine waited for Dan to chuckle but he didn't. That had obviously been the choice available. Blaine showing up again fitter but white could be explained away after a long absence. A change of ethnicity could not.

"He is all signed up and ready. If you ask me he must have landed on his head a few times but apparently he is legally sane and thinks he can beat the cancer through diet and exercise. He feels obligated to the ex-wives and the kids and who are we to argue."

"I know this is all a shock and has hit you all of a sudden but I need an answer as soon as possible. There is a lot to organise on our side and you'll have to break the news to Beth and the kids one way or another. I have cancelled your scheduled commitments for the next month. I suggest you take the rest of today to think it over. If necessary sleep on it tonight and let me know first thing tomorrow. I wouldn't like it to take any longer to come back to me with an answer."

But there was no need. Blaine had made up his mind. Dying didn't appeal and if some poor sucker was prepared to take over his health problems then more fool him. Who knows; maybe he could beat it with diet and exercise. That would be his problem.

"Let's go for it Dan. I'll need to let Beth and the kids know I'm ill but can get special treatment here which might save my life. If it works I'll tell her I've re-evaluated my life and decided to leave her. If it doesn't work out and I die then she doesn't need to know anything about that. Meanwhile I'll tell Delores the basics and get her on side. You happy with that?"

Dan looked at Blaine reassured that he was taking the whole thing remarkably well and would come out the other side ready to take the reins again and keep the money flowing.

"Sounds like a plan. I've got the jet here and we can fly back tonight. Delores can stay in England and tie in with Bobby. Don't cover too much with her at the moment. Bobby will brief her when she can see and believe the technology but only if it becomes really necessary. She'll stay with you through the whole shebang. Once you have told Beth and we have a date you'll fly back and join her. All being well you'll be sorted within a month or so and can run things from our European office while you recuperate and adjust. After six months or so you come back to headquarters, literally a new man. We can shuffle some of your closest staff about so nobody who knows you too well is there at that point. Give me a list of anyone we can dump too."

They both stood and shook hands. The older man held his grip and added, "Good luck son."

Chapter Seven

The next morning Frank woke at half six. Charlotte had headed back to her room about three in the morning but the bed still smelled of her perfume. What a night he thought and if Nebus didn't keep him too long each day he had the prospect of another two like it to look forward to. Still, work beckoned today and he better make a good first impression. A quick shower followed by a refreshing swim woke him up nicely. He was tired and could have slept a lot more but compared to waking up with one of his old hangovers this was a breeze.

He had a big healthy breakfast majoring in fruit and cereals which would give him energy throughout the day ahead. His previous experience, which was actually with some medical outfit retained by Nebus, involved a lot of time in the gym including days where food was reduced or even missing. The study had been about many things but part of it involved energy storage and retention. Frank had been starving by the end of some of the sessions and was planning ahead this time round. He looked round for Charlotte, but there was no sign. She had mentioned an early start and he assumed she had either made it or was sound asleep, exhausted in her room upstairs. He smiled thinking it was probably the latter but he really didn't care. Her life; her problem.

After breakfast he changed into a business like ensemble of smart jeans and his new a jacket, packed his sports bag with the tools of his trade and headed to the foyer to wait for his lift.

At ten past nine a skinny youth in scruffy jeans, tee-shirt and trainers walked through the entrance doors and straight up to Frank.

"Mr. Chisholm?" he inquired, putting out his hand to shake Frank's. Frank stood up and shook the hand, making sure it would hurt for a while afterwards.

"I'm David Simpson." Then after a pause and with slight embarrassment suggesting the title was a fairly recent acquisition he wasn't quite used to yet, "Dr David Simpson, Nebus Bioscience."

Frank was surprised and didn't manage to hide it.

David added, "Don't worry, it throws everyone. I'm 29 but still get ID'd in pubs."

Frank smiled his best friendly smile and added, "No kidding. So what are you a doctor of?" he asked with genuine interest.

"Well I'm a medical doctor first off then I have a PhD in....," he looked at Frank to gauge how technical to be. "Basically using computers in medicine," he précised, hitting the target audience perfectly.

"Like, using computers to analyse me in the gym?"

"Exactly, but taking it further with analysis of all aspects of peoples' health and brain functions. Looking for patterns that are measurable and can contribute to early diagnosis and treatment of illnesses being the main area I'm working on. Exercising yes, but also sleeping, eating, walking, reading. Basically recording and analysing the brain in all its activities. That's what you are here for. We like the results of your previous tests and want to take those further. I'll be running the day to day stuff with you, under the overall guidance of the center's Director, Dr Robert Bartleman. I think you spoke to him on the phone?"

"He's the yank," said Frank.

"Yep, Yank's okay," he confided," but don't use the term 'septic'. I find them a bit touchy about that nickname. He's okay and everyone calls him Bobby anyway. He is a genuine genius by the way. Even I struggle to keep up with him at times."

David led the way to a shiny people carrier which was waiting outside. It had blacked out windows and inside was a driver in a blazer who could have been the brother of Bob from the Prestwick private car company. The driver nodded and smiled at Frank who nodded and smiled back. The vehicle pulled off smoothly once they were all in and the seatbelts fastened, heading out of the hotel and away from the airport in the tail-end of the rush hour traffic round Edinburgh.

Frank was liking the sound of all this more and more. He had been ready for three weeks intensive in the gym but by the sound of it he was going to have a much easier time of it. He would be wired for sound right enough most of the time but if all he had to do was eat, sleep and shit... well he had managed all of that for years without being paid for it. This David guy seemed to be cool about the whole thing and if he was in charge of most of it then Frank had a pretty leisurely time ahead.

"Although you are booked into the Hilton for three weeks you will have to sleep over at the research centre for some of the testing sessions", said David.

A sudden alarm bell rang in Frank's head thinking of Charlotte from Carshalton. "When would that start?" he asked, sounding as nonchalant as possible.

"Probably the middle of week two, I guess," said David. "Most of the first week will be medicals, and calibrating the instruments. Today is mainly meeting the team and a full medical. Hope you don't mind a slow start. The guys we are working with are a good crowd. You'll like them; two guys from MIT and two from Belfast. One of the yanks calls himself Irish though."

 "Result!" thought Frank. A slow start would be fine for him after his nocturnal activities last night and by the sound of it there would be no interruptions to his plans for the next two nights either.

As they drove round the bypass to avoid Edinburgh itself David kept going with his run down of the weeks ahead. Franks results from before had indicated a very strong determination which was of particular interest to David. He was researching the link between brain activity and physical health and was hoping to find a correlation between strong will within the brain's function and a resulting process of health improvement. In simple terms, was it possible for the brain to improve physical health by wanting to do so?

Frank had listened to the start of it with interest but as the child doctor warmed to his subject Frank got left behind. He looked out of the window as they made their way slowly round the bypass in the heavy traffic. They passed a sign for Redford and Dreghorn barracks and Frank recognised the area from years back when he had been involved in The Edinburgh Military Tattoo and had been quartered in Redford Barracks. What a drafty shithole that had been he remembered. Not a patch on the Hilton.

After what seemed an age but had only been about 40 minutes they arrived at a large and prosperous looking business park on the South side of Edinburgh and pulled up in the car park of a plush unit with a tasteful sign at the entrance which read, Nebus Bioscience. It might as well have said money no object, thought Frank. The unit itself was immaculate with a manicured lawn round the sides which were visible to Frank. There was a water feature in front of the door with a luscious selection of exotic looking plants growing in and around the large pond. A fountain shot up about a metre in the middle and a waterfall babbled quietly in amongst the plants at one end. There were seats dotted here and there around the pond and in the grassy areas to the sides. A footpath snaked its way in and about the whole garden feature, presumably allowing Dr David and his guys thinking space when they needed it.

"I'm impressed," said Frank who was very impressed. "This looks like a high rent district."

"Actually Nebus Bioscience owns it lock stock and two smoking barrels. Or Bobby's uncle does which is the same thing as far as I can make out. You'll meet him while you're here. He's due in the middle of your third week. He scares the shit out of me to be honest but spends most of the time with Bobby talking about the American defence contracts they run here. It's all in a separate section of the plant which I don't have access to. That's where the money comes from to pay for this I gather. Certainly doesn't come from any of my work yet."

As they left the people carrier "Bob's brother" nodded a friendly farewell, checked his watch and took a paperback thriller out of the glove compartment. They walked over to the entrance and through the silent automatic doors to reception. A young scots girl sat behind the desk beside a large man in a uniform which said security on the sleeves. His haircut and broken nose said ex-forces and he eyed Frank up and down with more attention than most visitors got.

The girl smiled at Dr David and welcomed Frank to Nebus Bioscience and hoped he would enjoy his stay. She issued him with a badge which said visitor and had been prepared in advance. In small type the badge read "access areas A, B and C only." As easy as ABC thought Frank absently as he stared down the front of the girl's blouse. Her badge let the world know she was called Fiona and Frank had said, "Thank you Fiona," as he took his badge from her. He had seen no hint of interest from her but then he was here for three weeks. Plenty of time to wear her down.

"What's in A, B and C sections," he asked David.

"Everything but D section. That's the defence stuff. Don't worry about it. You can go anywhere in the plant that your card will open. D section has secure doors and two security guys there at all times. You'll probably never see it. It's nothing to do with why you're here anyway. Let's go and meet the guys you'll be working with."

Frank was starting to warm to Doc David. He looked like a school kid but had an air of confidence about him which suggested he knew his stuff inside out. The other thing Frank had noticed was David's lack of interest in his army days. Dr Johnson or Boswell or maybe it had been Paddy had once said "a man thinks less of himself for never having been a soldier." The upshot of that for Frank was a lot of questions from guys over the years about army life. He had also had to sort out the occasional military fantasist, all of whom seemed to have served in the SAS, when they tried to slag him off. Christ he thought, the SAS would be the biggest regiment in the British Army if they were all being honest. He liked sorting them out.

David had asked him no questions what so ever about the Paras, the army, guns, killing people or any of that usual shit. In other words he wasn't interested in it. His enthusiasm was all directed at his work and Frank's involvement in it, which David was looking forward to. Maybe he was gay Frank thought, but here too, there had been no obvious interest.

David led the way up a staircase from the reception desk towards an open canteen area above. There, at a table, were four youngsters, two lads and two girls. David made straight for them and they stood up as he approached.

"Meet the guys," he said and introduced them to Frank one at a time.

Frank was relieved that David used the term "guys" to include two girls, one of whom was quite tasty. The other reminded him of Velma from Scooby Doo. The attractive one may not have been Daphne, but she would certainly do on a quiet night as far as Frank was concerned. He noted her name was Bernadette, from Belfast and wondered what she would think about his two tours of Northern Ireland but, hey, hopefully we were all friends now after all. Frank had grown up telling racist, sexist and sectarian jokes like everyone else he knew in the west of Scotland. Like the rest of the country, though, he had travelled a journey of tolerance and discovery to the point where he would have objected to any jokes against somebody's race or religion. Sexism was work in progress with Frank but he was giving it his best shot. Hopefully he was ready to chat up Bernadette whatever her views on the troubles might be.

Velma turned out to be called Shona and the two boys were Jon without an 'H' and Brian. They both looked like shaggy but could have looked like Scooby Doo for all Frank cared. They all shook his hand and in fairness Frank didn't try to hurt theirs. They seemed a nice bunch who were looking forward to wiring Frank up to their computers. That was fine by him and Bernadette was a potential bonus after Charlotte legged it back to Carshalton. Maybe even before, but why be greedy. If he had a few sleep-overs coming up at the research facility, why not spend them with Bernie holding his hand. What was recorded on the computers as a result was not his problem. Maybe David could even use the data to cure people of something.

After a reasonable cup of coffee and some impressive home baking, David said he had stuff to do but asked Jon without an 'H' to show him round. Not fucking Jon, thought Frank. He'd never liked Shaggy and didn't want a grand tour from him now, even if Dr Bartleman turned out to be the Ghost after all. Fortunately Jon wasn't up for it either. Apparently he was behind reprogramming something needed for Frank's visit and needed to head straight back.

Great, one down two other ugly fuckers to go. He smiled at Daphne; sorry her name was Bernadette he corrected himself. She looked slightly shy as she returned his gaze but came up trumps by telling David that she was up to date with her analysis of his previous results and could give him the tour. David sounded genuinely grateful as he thanked her and asked Jon to get a move on with his programming.

"Aye and try to find yourself a fucking H for your name," thought Frank, chuckling to himself.

"Right Mr Chisholm, do you want a quickie or the full works," asked Bernadette with no sign of irony in her voice.

"Oh the full works please," said Frank with a wink which he thought might have been lost on young Bernie. "And Mr Chisholm was my father who died some time ago. Call me Frank."

Bernie used the name from then on but said it with reluctance as if she may well have regarded him as a father figure. If she had been studying his results from the previous study she would know that he wasn't anybody's typical father but maybe he could work on her as the weeks progressed.

They went from the cafeteria/restaurant back down the stairs to reception and started a grand tour of Nebus Bioscience's Scottish research facility. It was all impressive to Frank who even took his eyes off Bernie's skinny little arse for some of the time. To the right of reception was a corridor with offices off on both sides. She pointed out her own office which was labeled Dr Bernadette MacGuinness. Well, well thought Frank, so much for his picture of her in the typing pool. As it turned out there was no typing pool. The offices were where the team went to catch up on their own work or analyse results they had worked on together, she had explained. Each had their own specialisation she continued and had been head-hunted by Nebus from their respective Universities as being the best in their own field. It turned out that Velma and both Shaggies were Doctors too. You live and learn Frank thought.

After the offices they headed left at the far end of the corridor into an open space with the type of science desks Frank remembered from school but without the vandalism and graffiti. Science hadn't interested him then and he was not surprised to find nothing had changed.

Partly it was clear that none of his new, young friends worked in this section. Secondly nothing exciting appeared to be happening at any of the desks. No test-tubes, no Bunsen burners and no water taps. None of the toys Frank had been disciplined for playing with at school.

The tour continued with Bernadette leading him on another left turn and down a corridor with doors on either side. The doors were all windowless and designated as suites. The Penicuik suite turned out to be David's pad and Bernadette opened the door using her card.

"Your card will open this too and any other place you need to get into," she said as she held the door open for him. Inside Brian and David were sitting at computer terminals and Velma (or Shona) was checking over a collection of leads ranged round what looked like a cross between a hospital bed and a mortuary slab. They all looked up, shouted "Hi" and then got back to their own tasks. Bernadette took Frank round the room, explaining each piece of apparatus in turn. When she reached the bed she explained that this was where the calibration of the equipment would be carried out but once that was done he would have a mobile version on his back which he should get used to wearing. This would provide the volume of data they required as he carried out a wide range of activities. The Penicuik suite comprised a range of rooms including a fully equipped gym, changing facilities and a bedroom set up, which frank was disappointed to note had an enormous one way mirror viewable from an adjoining room. When she had finished the tour of this room she turned to David and asked what else she should cover.

He checked the clock and said: "Shit, Frank's due to meet Doctor Gibson in five minutes. Best get him over there pronto."

"Let's go," she said and led the way the way out of the suite and along the corridor to the end where she opened a door and headed across a broad hallway to another door requiring the use of her card. On the right of the hallway, Frank noticed a large desk with another useful looking security guard sitting behind it. His badge said Greg but nothing else.

Again Frank was eyed up and assessed with more interest than usual although the guard nodded and smiled a professional smile. If Frank had got this far with that skinny doctor he must be meant to be here. Either way he wasn't trying to get into D section which the man guarded with a well-paid concern. That meant Frank was none of his business. As the skinny doctor passed through the door with the new guy who looked like a boxer, the guard's colleague returned with two coffees in Nebus mugs.

"Did I miss anything?" he asked as he returned and placed one of the mugs in front of his colleague.

"New guy getting shown around. Bit of a hard case by the look of him. Guess he isn't a boffin but who knows. That skinny Irish lass with the flat chest is showing him the ropes. Thanks for the coffee mate."

Chapter Eight

Blaine headed back to his room and phoned Delores on his cell phone.

"Hi D, fancy coming over to my place? I've ordered some champagne on the company's tab and don't fancy drinking it alone. We need to talk."

"What about Dan?" asked Delores.

"Forget about Dan. He's busy in his room and will be all afternoon." He would tell her when she had arrived that Dan knew about them and didn't give a monkey's at the moment. If he told her any earlier she would be worried for her job and he had other bombshells to drop.

The Estonian waiter arrived with the champagne and two glasses at the exact moment that Delores arrived at Blaine's door. The waiter didn't bat an eyelid. He'd seen it all before with bosses and their secretaries. He hadn't seen it packaged quite as well as this secretary but he was professionally trained in his home country and kept a friendly air about his delivery without any winking or nudging in his comments or actions.

"Thanks bud," said Blaine, handing him a twenty pound note in his haste to get Delores alone.

The waiter took it with genuine thanks. Tips were pooled for all staff to share but not this one he thought. With a last sneaky look at Delores as he headed for the door he thought to himself, "lucky old bastard."

Delores rose to her feet once the waiter had left and kissed Blaine passionately on the lips. She looked worried and he was touched to note from her manner that it had nothing to do with the possibility of losing her job.

"Tell me what's happening Blaine," she pleaded. "We shouldn't risk meeting like this while Dan is still here."

Blaine handed her a glass of Champagne which she took with a look of confusion.

"Dan knows," he said gently, "and probably has done for some time. It is not important to him at the moment for a number of reasons. He is more concerned about losing me and my money making ability because I'm ill."

"How ill are you?" asked Delores with real concern in her voice.

"I have cancer and it is pretty well established," Blaine replied after a brief pause. "The only chance I have is an experimental procedure available here in Scotland. Dan's nephew Dr Robert Bartleman is the leading man in this field and is primed and ready to go. It is risky but he and Dan are convinced it will be successful. Either way I don't have much choice. Dan has set everything up and it can happen within a week or two."

Blaine stopped Delores from saying anything as he knew what he wanted to say and didn't want his flow interrupted. He was tired and knew he only had enough energy to go through this once. Then he would need to get his strength back to go through similar with Beth and the kids.

"Dan knows about us. I told him I wanted to come clean with all concerned and if things go well to set up a new home life with you. I need to know if that is what you want too."

Delores looked at him, taken aback by everything he had said.

"I want to be with you for good. Yes," she said. "If you want that I want it too. What about your wife? What about the children?"

"I'll tell Beth and the children. It's over with her and I'll see the children as often as I can which should be more often than at moment, especially if we aren't touring the world half the year."

"Are you sure about what you are saying. You might get bored if we are together openly. Maybe it won't be as exciting. We both need to be 100% sure before breaking up your family."

"I will never be bored with you. No man could be but I want to get well again and spend a lifetime with you."

Blaine meant it as he said it. "Dan won't be keen to have us working together. Too cosy he would say."

"I know but if we are going ahead with this I am going to choose your next PA and she will be old or ugly or preferably both."

Blaine laughed and gave her a long, lingering kiss on the lips. More champagne was needed and poured and they laughed and joked for a while, all tension released for the moment.

Then they made love. Not the greatest ever they agreed but Blaine was tired and Delores knew it. The act had been a necessary sealing of their bargain if nothing else. Afterwards Blaine laid out the plans for the next few weeks and Delores, although disappointed at not being with Blaine initially was pleased it would be her who nursed him through what lay ahead. All of it with Dan's blessing it seemed.

Blaine fell asleep after that and Delores tucked him up in bed realising he needed his rest now. She kissed him gently on the forehead and went back to her room to think through everything she had just learned. Blaine's illness was a blow it was true but she had known for some time that something wasn't right. Now she had the details, bad as they were, she could plan and help him now as never before. The prize was there too of being with him for good, without having to skulk about all the time fearful of discovery and the ten o'clock walk when Dan found out.

She wasn't tired and certainly couldn't have slept. She decided to go for a swim in the hotel pool and found the activity a pleasantly relaxing experience. Afterwards she headed for her room intending to have a nap herself before meeting Blaine for dinner. Dan Bartleman had other plans. When she opened the door there was a hand written note from him asking her to join him in the lounge when she got the message. He was a stickler for protocol with female employees and would never have invited her to his room alone. Doc Zelnik had headed off to Edinburgh for a meeting she now realised was with young Bobby Bartleman and no other chaperone was available. She dressed in smart but business-like clothes and headed for the bar. She was nervous, which was unusual, but this meeting was different to any she had before with Blaine's boss. The capo di capo they would call him when they were alone together. It was said with respect. At most meetings she had attended where Dan was present she was there merely as Blaine's PA Blaine dealt with everything thrown at him like the able CEO he was. Any questions addressed to her were usually to do with facts, figures and dates. Now Dan wanted to see her on her own. About her future and she was scared to face it without Blaine at her side.

Dan was there in a corner seat working on his laptop and phone simultaneously. He was engrossed and didn't notice her enter the lounge bar at first. When her shoes were in his line of sight he looked up and smiled at her. It seemed to be a friendly smile of concern but she kept her guard up. He abruptly terminated his phone call and rose to his feet, taking her hand and directing her to the chair immediately to his right. She knew this was his better ear.

"Has Blaine explained his situation my dear?" he asked with what seemed like genuine concern in his voice.

"Yes he has," she answered, in a more confident voice than she had expected. Blaine's promise had given her strength.

"Good. Now tell me your understanding of the situation. Blaine and I discussed this in detail earlier. I want to make sure you are on the same wavelength as the two of us. To reassure you, I am pleased the two of you are," he searched for the right term, "an item, shall we say. Blaine is very ill and I am very keen to help him get well in any way I can, for all sorts of reasons. I believe he wishes you to be with him during his forthcoming treatment and," at this he studied Delores carefully for her reaction, "at the other end of things on a more permanent footing."

She didn't blink. "Yes that is my understanding of the situation too. I gather the treatment is somewhat experimental and there are risks involved but I want to help Blaine too and will be by his side every step of the way. He is going to tell Beth about the illness next and about us in due course after the treatment is completed if it is succesful. I am comfortable with that approach."

"Good," said Dan. "Blaine is a lucky man you know. I hope you will be very happy together when all this is over with. In the meantime of course you remain an employee of Nebus. In other words I expect you to keep anything you discover about the treatment a secret. It is beyond share-sensitive. I have to emphasise this point. Whatever you learn about the treatment Blaine is about to undergo must remain a secret. This is more important than any duty you have undertaken in your employment to date. Do I make myself clear? Any disclosure would leave you liable to legal action and could jeopardise Blaine's position within the company too. Be clear on that also."

Delores was not entirely sure why Dan was emphasising this point so much. She had never even considered disclosing what she heard or saw in her daily duties to any outside person. Her focus now was certainly not on industrial espionage. It was on Blaine and nothing else. She nodded and confirmed she understood the importance of it and would never do anything to jeopardise Blaine's future or breach the trust placed in her and she meant it.

Dan stared at her reassuring himself that the threat to Blaine would keep her focussed on this point and saw that it would. He relaxed and smiled again.

"Sorry to be a pain but I had to cover that. Will you join me for a drink?"

The old man seemed much more relaxed to Delores now and also seemed intent on being sociable. He called a waiter over and she ordered a gin and tonic while he ordered a Macallan. While they waited he chatted away about all sorts of things, including some tales of dodgy dealings in his youth as he made his fortune. He was actually quite good company she thought, once he finally relaxed. He even ignored a number of calls on his mobile in order to deliver the punch lines of some of his stories. He asked her about her background and upbringing and was impressed at how far she had come from difficult circumstances. All in all he seemed to be a very different person from the one she had met chairing meetings before. She half expected him to ask her out, he was being so charming. But after a while she realised that he was relaxing after being quite stressed about Blaine's predicament. How touching she thought and warmed to him just a fraction.

When he had finished his drink he rose and said he had to make some calls in his room. In a very formal, old fashioned way he thanked her for her company and, picking up his phone and laptop headed towards the lift. As he was leaving the table though he stopped and turned towards her again.

"I know Blaine is in safe hands," he said, smiled at her, and headed off to his room.

"Well, well, well," she thought. "So the old bastard is human after all."

She finished her drink and, unusually for her, ordered another. She needed thinking time after all that had happened and knew Blaine had to sleep for a while or at least needed to rest even if he woke. She checked her phone and emails but there were none. Normally both would have been full after even an hour of not checking but strangely the only text was from her sister about a family get together she was organising later in the year. When Dan said he had cancelled Blaine's schedule he meant it. To stop the emails and phone calls to her as well was on a par with parting the Red Sea. After five minutes she realised waiting on her own with a second drink had been a mistake. Unused to being in a bar without Blaine or other male colleagues she had forgotten how every bar-fly in Christendom had been drawn to her. Clearly unaccompanied, she had attracted the attention of every male in the place even, or perhaps especially, the two married men with their wives. Two sales reps in High Street suits approached and asked if she would like some company. A gun would have been preferable she thought.

"No thank you," she said with a smile that was not in any way friendly or inviting. "I'm waiting for my husband. He'll be here soon."

They nodded and walked off to the bar, one of them with a shrug suggesting it was her loss. She was pretty sure it wasn't. She downed the last of her second gin and tonic and headed back to check on Blaine. There was no response to her gentle tap on the door so she quickly scribbled a note saying she would wait in her room and slipped it underneath.

Back in her own room she tried to take stock of what had happened. She was always in control of her reactions when people were about. It was part of the job of an unflappable PA to take everything in her stride but all this was overwhelming. Blaine being ill was top of the bombshells which had been dropped. Thereafter most of what she had based her working life upon recently had been blown out of the water too. It was one thing to have a long term relationship with your married boss when it was a secret and that was all it was likely to be. Now she had the option of it becoming a lifetime commitment and that scared her more. Yes; if she was honest she did love Blaine. It had all started as a measure of the distance she had travelled from her childhood poverty but it had grown beyond that now. She did not want to break up any family but if that was a charade anyway then she would prefer to be honest about it all and people could think what they wanted to. Strangely she felt reassured by Dan's audience with her that night. He was a wily old bastard, intent on getting even richer than he currently was for no good reason she could see. But having such a powerful ally on their side made the future with Blaine a much stronger and more tangible possibility. Either way, most of the decision making was outwith her control. She wanted Blaine to live. Tick. She wanted to spend her life with him if possible. Tick. An option was available for that to happen and Dan was prepared to make it happen. Tick. The rest kind of took care of itself.

She showered again for no reason and put on a negligee. Secretly she thought Blaine would sleep and not appear that night and maybe she wanted that too but she wanted to be ready for him if he came to her room. She lay down in her bed, suddenly exhausted and quickly fell asleep. If Blaine had appeared at her door she might have missed his knock, so soundly did she sleep, but he did not. In his room he slept the sleep of the dead. Or not quite dead.

Chapter Nine

Dr Gibson's office was at the end of another corridor which had a variety of laboratories ranged along it. Some had clear glass on the doors and through the windows Frank saw some cages containing mice, monkeys, rats and other creatures Frank didn't recognise.

The doctors consulting room was as different from Frank's own doctor's as he could imagine. No paperwork or paper files anywhere. It was a very large room with a lot of very new and very expensive looking equipment ranged round the walls. In fact, it looked like Gibson could successfully perform heart surgery without leaving his office.

"Sorry we're late," said Bernadette as they entered.

Dr Gibson didn't look like he was over-worked or rushing for anything any time soon. He had some results to check but was leaving them as a treat for later or even tomorrow. The working day was a very relaxed affair for him. Occasional annual medicals, some researchers asking his opinion on medical matters every now and then and the odd headache or two which hadn't gone away with a standard painkiller. That was about it really. No, filling his day could be the real hard work. This afternoon was rather nicely filled with meeting Mr Frank

Chisholm Esq. and starting an exhaustive series of examinations and tests which should take care of tomorrow afternoon too. They had even arrived a little late, using up another 15 minutes of this Monday.

"No need to apologise Bernie," he said with complete honesty.

She said her farewells to Frank and left. He'd smiled and said see you later in a kind of questioning way to gauge her first impressions of him but could read nothing into her response.

"Now then, I'm Dr John Gibson and please call me John."

The two men shook hands and Frank found an equally firm handshake neutralising his best efforts to hurt the Doc's hand. Dr John Gibson was about 60 or so and looked it but had the still powerful frame of someone who had been a keen athlete in their younger days. Not boxing Frank judged from the unbroken nose but a power sport of some kind. A photograph on the wall behind the doctor's desk suggested field athletics. No doubt shot-put or discus.

John continued in a slow and friendly bedside manner explaining the nature of his duties over the next few days.

"I will be conducting a full medical examination with every test any doctor has ever done on you and many that they haven't. There are also a number of detailed health questionnaires which my nurse, Moira, will complete with you. If there is anything you find too embarrassing to discuss with her we can sort it out together but she has been a nurse for almost 40 years and has seen it all."

Frank's heart sank a bit at the likely age of nurse Moira but then there were still possibilities with Bernie or Fiona at reception. Oh, and of course for the next few days at least, Charlotte from Carshalton on the nightshift.

Doc Gibson ran through the personal details they held on Frank from his previous test session. Then he said he would start with the basics; pulse-rate, height, weight, that sort of thing. Frank had been through this stuff so often before, during and after his military service, that it had become routine. Dr Gibson measured, double checked and recorded all the results on the tablet he had produced from his desk. The examination continued with Frank slowly stripping off more layers.

"Need a pee yet?" Gibson asked holding out a specimen jar.

"Could do," said Frank taking it and heading for the door marked toilet.

He returned shortly afterwards with a jar full of pee and handed it to the doctor. Gibson took it gingerly, noting that it had drops of urine on the outside too. Frank had never quite got the hang of that one and had headed back into the toilet to give his hands a good wash.

Next some blood was taken and split into a number of small test-tubes which had already been labeled with Frank's name and had barcodes neatly down the side of each label. The examination wore on and on with Frank lying down, bending over and bracing himself in turn while Doc Gibson, "please it's John", poked, prodded and violated every orifice.

Eventually he was done or at least done for the day. Frank got fully dressed again.

"I meant to ask earlier, have you had lunch? Your stomach seemed quite empty during the examination."

Frank had not had lunch and was quite impressed the old guy had noticed by that method.

"No I seem to have missed it out but I had a good breakfast at the hotel this morning," he said having completely forgotten about food, what with all the poking, prodding and discussions about bodily functions and fluids.

"Would you like a bite to eat now, it's almost three o'clock?"

"I could do with something light to keep me going till dinner at the restaurant tonight. I'll need some energy for the gym and a swim when I get back."

"Of course. Sorry about that." Dr Gibson pressed a button on his desk and a lady about ages with him entered from an adjoining door. "This is my wife Moira who is also the plant nurse."

Frank shook her hand.

"Moira, would you mind taking Mr Chisum to the canteen. I seemed to have made him miss lunch.

Moira nodded and gave her husband a look that said "typical" in an affectionate way as she led Frank back out the main office door, round a corner, past reception and up the stairs to the canteen.

Frank had visions of a half empty cold section with a few tired sandwiches and the cakes and scones which no one else fancied but he was pleasantly surprised to find fresh home baking again on tables with a number of people sitting in groups chatting away in a very unhurried atmosphere.

Moira turned to him and asked: "Would you like anything cooked? I'll organise it with the chef or would you prefer some home baking with coffee?"

"A sandwich of some kind with lettuce, tomato and some dead animal would be nice," he said. "If it doesn't piss the chef off too much."

"He'll be delighted to have something to do. He is on call for fresh food outwith standard meal times till five so have what you want. His Caesar salad is very good."

"A ham sandwich would be perfect thanks and I'll drink some fruit juice instead of coffee," Frank added noting some jugs in the cold section with fresh apple, orange and tomato juice in them. He helped himself to a large glass of chilled apple juice.

Moira trotted off to the kitchen while Frank looked round to see if there was anyone he recognised. Brian was sitting at a table with Jon but that was it. He wasn't keen but felt obliged to join them. After all, they would be working together over the next few weeks.

"Hi guys," he said. "Mind if I join you?"

"Not at all," they both replied almost in unison.

"How was your tour?" asked Brian with what seemed like genuine interest.

"Impressive place you have here," said Frank and meant it. "Bernie showed me round the place. It was going well till I met Doc Gibson and he really took the piss."

Frank laughed at the old army chestnut and after a moment's pause the lads joined in. They gave him a breakdown of how the preparations were going for the calibration tomorrow morning. All seemed to have gone well with the preparations that day and they were hopeful it would be a successful start to the testing the next day.

Moira arrived with an immaculately prepared roast ham and salad club sandwich with a side salad created by a sculptor rather than a chef.

"I told you the chef would be happy to prepare anything you wanted. Enjoy! I'll see you tomorrow afternoon and you can tell me all about your ill spent youth for the first of the questionnaires." She winked and left him with Brian and Jon.

"Moira's really nice," said Brian. "Bit of a mother hen to the younger staff here like me and Jon. You can ask her pretty much anything you're worried about."

Frank wasn't sure what either of them might be worried about regarding their health but he was convinced he didn't want to know. He ate the sandwich while they continued to brief him on what they had been up to since his visit to the Penicuik suite. They talked enthusiastically about things he had no understanding of. While they talked he enjoyed his sandwich. The ham was beautifully home cooked, probably by the chef himself. There was Dijon mustard there too and the salad had a delicate French dressing, no doubt "drizzled" over it. Again, it had to have been home made by a bored chef keen to impress. Let the lads talk he thought and keep the food coming and these three weeks will be a breeze.

After he was finished the sandwich and there was a pause in the conversation he asked them what was next for him. They looked at him fairly blank.

"If the Doc's finished with you then you're done for today," said Brian.

"Really. That was all painless and easy for the first day. How do I get back to the hotel?"

"Just get Jim to drive you back. He should be waiting in the car park. He'll be your transport each day."

Frank was impressed again but this time by how important he must be to get all this special treatment. He said his good-byes, picked up his, as yet un-needed, sports bag and headed for the stairs.

"You won't need that this week," shouted Jon. Without looking round Frank gave him a thumbs up and took the stairs two at a time. He smiled a farewell at Fiona on reception who seemed to have warmed to him a bit and smiled back with a friendly wave.

Out in the car park Bob, no it was Jim here wasn't it, was sitting in the people carrier reading his thriller but put it down immediately when Frank opened the passenger door.

"Hi. Where to?" asked Jim with a friendly smile.

"Take me to The Hilton please. I feel a dip in the pool coming on," replied Frank with a smile. He was loving this now he'd seen the place and knew what lay ahead, none of which seemed to be very demanding.

Jim started up the engine and pulled smoothly out of the car park towards the main road. The two men traded small talk about football on the return journey. Slagging off each other's teams as only a Hearts fan and a Rangers fan could do in Scotland i.e. with relative neutrality. They were early enough to beat the rush hour on the by-pass and made better time than on the outward journey. Jim pulled up at the Hilton and Frank jumped out.

"I've to collect you tomorrow at nine if that's okay," he asked.

Sounded fine to Frank. "See you then."

He went into the hotel and asked if there were any messages for him. He didn't expect any but he had always wanted to do that in a posh hotel. After a quick search the young lad behind the desk apologised and confirmed there were none with a genuine hint of disappointment in his voice.

"No worries," reassured Frank and headed to his room. He knew Charlotte from Carshalton wouldn't be back till after six o'clock and they had arranged to have dinner again around eight. That gave him plenty of time for a quick nap, a swim and a shower before then. The club sandwich had filled him up and he felt it deserved an hour or so to settle in his stomach before being taken for a swim. He'd give the chef plenty of work over the next three weeks and see how he did.

He slept too late for the swim and guessed last night's activities had taken more out of him than he had realised.

"Getting old my son," he thought but didn't believe it or care. He was still in time for the shower and to try out some more of his glad rags for the dinner with Charlotte.

The evening followed a very similar pattern to the previous one except they stayed for coffee and tried Charlotte's room for size. Frank headed for his room about two o'clock in the morning and slept like a log. Life was good.

Chapter Ten

Breakfast the next day was a strangely cheerful event. Dan's good humour of the evening before had survived both the night and a few troublesome business phone calls. Blaine and Delores were able to relax in each other's company in public for the first time, even with Dan there. No discussion took place regarding what lay ahead. All decisions had been made now and there was no going back. Instead it was a case of enjoying every moment life gave them together. Even Dan had relaxed to the point of discussing even more of his shady past with Blaine, for everyone's amusement more than anything else. They ate, they laughed and they enjoyed the last breakfast together before the plan had to take effect.

When they were finished Dan excused himself and headed for his room but not before giving a strict timetable for Blaine to be ready to take the corporate jet back to the States. Blaine and Delores talked about anything but what was important and then, with no time to consummate their planned future again, headed off to their rooms for their very different destinations. Before they left the restaurant they kissed a passionate and full kiss on the lips for anyone to see who wanted to. They had a future together and Dan's permission to enjoy it to the full and nothing would take them back to their old furtive ways. That kiss was also a secret agreement that they both had separate ways to travel over the next few weeks but would stay in touch spiritually throughout.

They both went to their respective rooms and packed. Delores had a private car booked for two o'clock that afternoon, two hours after Blaine and Dan had taken off from Prestwick Airport for their trip back to the States. She would have a week or so with Bobby Bartleman in Edinburgh before Blaine returned at which point she could focus her entire attention on him and his wellbeing for the first time ever. The initial itinerary had her booked into the Edinburgh Airport Hilton but Dan had changed that to a more central serviced flat in Edinburgh. Delores was pleased. That would be a better venue for nursing Blaine back to health and the last thing she needed was a week of fighting off bar-room Casanovas who were all War Heroes or Boxing champions or similar and wanted her notch on their bed post. She could do without that.

Just before 2 pm, she got a call to say her transport was waiting for her. A local youth with spots and very little arm strength appeared to carry her bags down to reception. It was a summer job for him before studying horticulture at the local Agricultural College and he struggled not to stare at Delores backside and breasts in the lift as they made their descent to reception. She was uncomfortably aware of his attention but in the great scheme of things it was small beer. She knew she could kill him if he got fresh and also knew he was so shy he would not. Either way, as long as he got her luggage to the car without dropping it she would be happy enough. If he did she might kill him anyway. Her luggage was too expensive to be careless with. Whatever happened, though, this kid had had his tip already.

A smart Audi estate from a local private hire company was waiting for her and her luggage. The driver introduced himself as John. He wasn't a regular driver with the company but covered dayshifts for the regulars and was standing in for Bob who had a dental appointment. Delores looked at him with a look that said, not unkindly she hoped, whatever and thanked the pimply youth for making it to the car without dropping anything but his jaw.

Off the car went with John and Delores towards Edinburgh. John was determined to impress and recounted the story of being phoned the day before and ordered (his words) to collect some VIP Americans earlier that morning and drive them to Prestwick Airport to catch a private jet bound for Nebraska. He waited for his gorgeous passenger to look suitably awed by his importance and was disappointed by her lack of interest. She was gorgeous he had realised and was headed to a private serviced flat in Edinburgh. From the thrillers he had read that suggested she might be a high class hooker. She was certainly pretty enough to be one. Aloof you might say. Either way, he suspected she might be out of his league although he mentally totalled up all his savings just in case.

The journey to Edinburgh passed without event as far as Delores was concerned although she found the chatter from her non-regular driver a bit annoying. He had pointed out land marks along the way to try to keep her interested. Harthill services which had once been the only service station to have a mention in the Egon Ronay guide. "The Pyramids" bizarre landscaping where Motorola's silicon glen involvement had ended and where sheep were now dyed various colours to amuse the passing commuters, whose jobs generally no longer had anything to do with electronics. A sculpture which looked like the Tellytubbies phone and various other local landmarks. Delores was bored but through politeness tried not to show it. John couldn't care less. He had the most beautiful woman in his car and he would talk about it for weeks afterwards with slowly reducing degrees of honesty.

The car arrived at the flat in a plush area of central Edinburgh and Delores met the concierge and let John carry the bags to the flat. She took the key, thanked John this time with a tip and headed for the sanctuary of the flat. Blaine had caught the private jet that morning with Dan and was probably still in the air heading for Nebraska. She felt as if her responsibilities were passed to Dan for the moment but knew they would resume soon enough. The serviced flat came with membership of a private gym which she was relieved to find had ladies only sessions throughout the week. She would rest and exercise while she waited for Blaine and could be sure of no unwelcome male stalkers in between. She had an appointment with Dr Robert Bartleman in three days' time and found a pass key for his research facility waiting for her in the flat which said access all areas; a,b,c and d. Sounded like she could have lunch with Mickey Mouse at no extra charge with this card. Either way she had a break now to gather her strength ready to support Blaine in whatever lay ahead.

In the Lear Jet at 30 something thousand feet Dan slept and Blaine did not. He was actually more positive and focussed than he had been for some time and it was that which was keeping him awake. He was very conscious of his mortality but also felt liberated by the limited hand which life had dealt him. He had to go home to see Beth and to break the news of his cancer to her. He knew she would be upset but would be stoic in her support of him and the kids' needs when they found out their father was seriously ill. In fact he knew in advance that his home-making wife would be exceptionally good at this side of things. In some ways he was pleased to have Beth supporting him at this point. Beth would keep the home-fires burning whatever happened and keep their kids focussed on softball, soccer or whatever they were into at the moment. He had a brief feeling of nostalgia from their early romance but tried to erase it from his mind in loyalty to Delores and their future together. Eventually he dosed off and slept soundly, dreaming not of domestic bliss but of impressive balance sheets and share options.

When he eventually got home things went pretty much as he had anticipated with Beth, who after a few tears, rallied and started planning and organising her support. She decided it would be better if she spoke to the kids. This was both brave and practical as she was the one who spent all her time looking after them. In honesty Blaine was almost a stranger to them. They looked forward to his time at home, on the rare occasions he was home while they were awake. They also looked forward to his return from business trips as he usually brought presents for them from wherever he had been. They remained completely unaware that almost all of them had been chosen by Delores. However, when it came down to something serious which could affect their domestic routine with mom, she was the one who could explain better to them in terms they would be able to understand. Clara was ten and took the news surprisingly well. Daniel who had just passed eight didn't fully understand but nodded when his mother explained that daddy was ill and had to go away for a while so they had to help her all they could. Had they been a bit older and therefore more cynical they might have asked: "So what's new?" Instead they nodded their differing levels of understanding and ran off to give daddy plenty of hugs and kisses as requested. Blaine was tired in a way he hadn't been for a very long time. As they ran up and grabbed him he was relieved that they were as gentle as Beth had asked them to be and for once let them give him as many hugs and kisses as they wanted. When they were done he sent them off to do their chores and dozed off in his favourite chair, feeling like an old man but unable to fight the fatigue any further.

When he awoke Daniel had made him a card which read, "Love you daddy.' Clara had picked him some flowers from their garden and for a second he almost shed a tear of emotion. Almost! He had a long way to go and at the end of it he would undoubtedly spend as much time as he could with the children but it wouldn't be here and it would be with Delores.

The next three days seemed to drag by until Dan phoned confirming a date had been agreed with the donor. Thereafter the house became a blur of activity with Beth in sole charge of everything that happened. This had allowed Blaine to phone and text Delores a few times, carefully deleting all contact afterwards on his cell phone. By agreement the contact was short and to the point.

The day came for Blaine to travel again in the private jet, this time to Edinburgh with Doc Zelnik as a travelling companion in case of any medical emergencies en route. Dan had telephoned the night before to wish Blaine luck and to confirm he would appear in Edinburgh towards the end of the process and personally take charge of the new Blaine's re-establishment within Nebus.

Dr Zelnik appeared in a company owned limo in plenty of time to collect Blaine and get to the airport. He spent a half hour or so checking him over medically and pronounced him fit to travel then said he would wait by the car till Blaine said his farewells to the his family.

The kids had been up early and had been scrubbed and polished by the maid to look their best. This had allowed Beth to do the same to herself. By agreement Blaine had moved to the guest room on the ground floor after the dates had been confirmed to allow him maximum rest and to avoid the stairs. He knew he could have managed them easily enough but the privacy gave him plenty of thinking time. The arrangement meant that Beth could focus that morning on looking as good as she possibly could. After her customary run and session on the exercise bike and cross trainer she had taken a relaxing bath. Thereafter, she had got dressed in a short summer dress bought specially for the occasion and taken the time to get her make up just right. The effect as she lined up the kids to say "Goodbye" to their father was exactly as she had hoped. Blaine looked at her and stopped just that split second. She looked beautiful. He smiled at her a genuinely warm and affectionate smile and gave her a long kiss full on the lips.

Before he could stop himself he said, "I love you," and meant it.

Beth smiled back and said, "You come safely back to me now! We'll all be waiting here for you and will be ready to spoil you till you're all better." She winked a surprisingly dirty wink as she said it and gave him another lingering kiss. After that, he gave first Clara and then Daniel long hugs and made them promise to help their mom all they could and be good. He then turned and walked slowly to the limo. Doc Zelnik had come up to the front door to help him if needed and they walked to the car side by side. The doctor opened the car door for the younger man who turned and blew a kiss to his family, wondering if this was the last time he would see them or if it would just be the last time they would all smile at him if things went according to plan. Either way, when he had settled into the back of the car and it had started for the airport, he realised for the first time in years the future was out of his hands for the next few weeks. He had no decisions to make, no meetings to chair and no immediate responsibilities for anyone else. Others were taking responsibility for him as never before since he was a child and it was a very strange but not an entirely unpleasant feeling. There would be difficult times ahead but for now he could switch off and let the fatigue envelope him. He had made his decisions and would stick to them as usual. Wavering was dangerous. Keep the long term prize in sight and go for it.

Chapter Eleven

The next day Frank bounced out of bed early enough to have a swim before breakfast, worrying that a week of no exercise at Nebus would mean he'd have to make up for it at the hotel. Charlotte was fun but not all of his muscle groups were getting a workout with her. Showered, fed and dressed in a jacket and jeans he was ready in reception when Jim pulled up in his people carrier.

"Wasn't sure if a Jambo would be on time," Frank joked.

"Can't trust a blue nose sitting about in my home town, get in."

And so began Frank's second day at Nebus. The morning was all about fitting electrodes to his head and getting him to sit up, stand up, sit down, lie down and so on. He felt like a dog getting trained but it was easy enough and he could pass the time thinking about the money he was getting paid, Charlotte or, when he could see her, Bernie's skinny bum. The kids seemed happy with the progress they had made by lunchtime and said they would work on the results in the afternoon. He could eat now and then it was off to see nurse Moira for two o'clock.

"You hungry," he asked Bernie as he passed her, ignoring the rest of the team.

"A bit. Give me just a few seconds to finish this programme and start it running then I'll join you if you like."

Frank liked, so he pulled up a chair and watched as she entered the last of her instructions into the PC, pretending all the time to be interested. Then they headed for the canteen. Once there they both ordered from the list of hot dishes available with Frank adding some special requests for his, just to cheer the chef up. He poured some apple juice and some for Bernie when she asked him and they sat down.

"So what is a nice girl like you doing in a place like this," Frank ventured.

Bernie looked at him for a second and then replied, "I have a PhD in Data processing and was head hunted by Nebus when I finished my doctorate." There was not a trace of a smile on her face.

"That went well," thought Frank for a second until Bernie burst out laughing.

"That is the most lame chat up line I have heard since High School," she said still laughing at the look of confusion on Frank's face.

"Okay, you got me that time," he said and joined in.

After that, with the ice broken they chatted away about the tests, the research at Nebus and then into the topic of Northern Ireland, with Frank on the defensive till he gauged her position. It turned out her position was simple. Get qualified, get out and see the world. The troubles hadn't really affected her family and she didn't give a monkey's that Frank had been a soldier there. He breathed a sigh of relief and turned up the charm to the "High" setting.

Their food arrived and again Frank was impressed by the chef's efforts. They ate in silence for a while and then resumed their conversation with coffees. Frank joked and smiled and gave it all he had in an attempt to make up for his lack of formal education. Bernie was about the brightest girl who'd ever sat and listened to him and he didn't want to blow it. Early on she had admitted to being single after a disastrous spell with a fellow PhD student, who had a drink problem, while they were both studying in Belfast. After that she had a few casual boyfriends but intended to get on and see the world. Settling down with anyone was not a priority and if it never happened she would not be bothered. Frank liked everything she said on the subject. Especially that word casual. But he took care to omit any mention of hard drinking in his own past after that.

"Fancy a bite to eat at my Hotel tomorrow night?" he asked casually.

She paused before replying with a smile, "We'll see how you perform tomorrow then I'll let you know. For now I need to get back to work and you need to tell Nurse Moira about all your spots and rashes."

He stood up as she left the canteen smiling a farewell. "Well well well," he thought. "Life just gets better and better."

He finished the last mouthful of his coffee which was by now stone cold and headed off to the medical suite.

As Doc "please call me John" Gibson had suggested, his wife had seen and heard it all before. Prior to joining Nebus, she had been a sister in the Accident and Emergency department of a large general hospital. Nothing Frank told her, in answer to her rather detailed questions, fazed her at all. Indeed after a while and some scary anecdotes from her he even started to think he might have led a rather sheltered life.

She was very easy to talk to and even when she started to major on his previous drinking habits he felt it quite natural to give her the unedited version, which wasn't pretty. As a result, she said they would be doing some extra tests and scans on his liver to assess the extent of any permanent damage and some of this would involve a visit to a local hospital.

"Private," she said with an element of distaste, "so plenty of staff and no queuing."

After what seemed an age she announced that she had finished for the day but that there would be further questionnaires once his answers had been analysed and also after the visit to the hospital. There would also be ongoing medical assessment during the three weeks to make sure he wasn't suffering any trauma.

"No trauma so far," he assured her as he left her office and headed to the canteen.

It was 3.30 and he was hungry again. He hoped he might meet up with Bernie again but she was nowhere to be seen. Indeed the canteen was very quiet. A couple of kids in lab coats and an assistant behind the counter. He asked her for a fairly challenging bite to eat to keep the chef occupied and made his way to an empty table carrying an orange juice. The guys in lab coats kept talking without acknowledging his arrival. That's fine, he thought, I wouldn't understand a word they're saying anyway.

The mature lady from behind the counter appeared with his savoury crepe with grilled mushrooms and gruyere cheese, accompanied by a salad of grated carrots, fresh low fat coleslaw and couscous. Again it looked fantastic and he tucked in.

Just as he was about to finish his plateful he looked and almost choked on a piece of crepe. The most beautiful woman he had ever seen had just walked into the canteen and had made her way to the counter. She was tall and slim with perfect dark skin and black hair. Her figure was incredible and Frank realised his mouth was wide open. "Not cool," he thought and closed it.

Stay calm my son. Act cool. Maybe she will sit beside the kids if she knows them or me if I'm unbelievably lucky. If she sits on her own I'll grab a coffee and join her. He watched her unashamedly as she ordered a coffee "to go" in a deep American accent with an educated southern drawl. Frank watched every movement she made. Imagined movements she didn't make. He had never seen anyone as beautiful before.

She took the coffee from the assistant and thanked her politely then walked back to the stairs and descended towards reception.

Frank was on his feet in a shot, all thoughts of finishing his plate or washing it down with a coffee now gone. This was far more important. He tried to appear as casual as possible as he too descended the stairs and followed her along a corridor. He would stay just a little behind her and see which office or suite she worked in. Then it should be a simple matter during the three weeks there to bump into her and give it the charm as only he could. He had some leaflets in his hand that nurse Moira had given him to read based on some of his answers to her questions and he pretended to read them in case she looked round. But she didn't. She had a distracted, almost worried look on her face and never noticed Frank stalking her.

She headed on down the corridor until she arrived at D section, walking straight in as one of the security guards smiled and opened the security door using a switch on his desk.

"Bugger," thought Frank.

That was going to make things a bit more difficult. One of the security guys eyed Frank suspiciously as he approached the desk but just at the last moment Frank looked up in a distracted way and turned down the corridor towards The Penicuik Suite. The guard watched him all the way till he turned a corner and was out of sight.

"They're good," he thought, "if they watch me with someone like her on their monitors."

The guard who had watched Frank turned to his buddy and said, "there's something strange about that guy, you know, the hard case working with the Irish lass."

His colleague didn't look up from his monitor. "Could still be a boffin though, reading stuff as he walks along the corridor. Bit of a giveaway wouldn't you say?"

"Can't be that bright though, reading a leaflet called 'How to tell if you have genital warts' for all the world to see," and they both laughed briefly before returning to their normal duties.

Frank made his way to the Penicuik Suite and went in for no good reason at all. Jon was there on his own working on some wiring which had been attached to Frank earlier. He hadn't even heard Frank come in and didn't look up. Frank left and headed off to reception the opposite route from D section. Fiona was not there only her security guard colleague who gave Frank a polite but slightly suspicious nod as he passed and made his way over to Jim and the people carrier. Frank realised he must stand out like a sore thumb amongst the boffins and whiz-kids at Nebus Biosciences and security, with very little else to do, were happy to eye him up and down whenever they saw him. He didn't much like it but supposed they were only doing their job. Still he wouldn't mind a chance to sort out that nosey one at D section. He would enjoy doing that.

"Home James, and don't spare the horses," he said to Jim with a smile. Charlotte awaits and with the lights out she might as well be the American vision of beauty he had just seen. He didn't know how but he was determined to see her again and try his luck. He hadn't figured out how yet but that was a mere detail. The way his luck was going at the moment he would get a chance one way or another.

When he arrived at the hotel he was surprised when the young lad behind the reception desk called his name and said: "I have a message for you tonight Mr Chisholm," and handed him an envelope with a note inside. Intrigued he opened it straight away and discovered it was from Charlotte. Apparently, she had to attend a night-out at the end of the course she was running and wouldn't be back before eleven o'clock at the earliest.

"Bugger," Frank thought of himself. She might be back around eleven or she might end up making a night of it and stagger in much later. He thanked the lad at reception and headed up to his room. A quick change and he was headed to the gym and the pool for a bit of a workout before dinner; a meal he looked destined to eat alone. It was on occasions like this that his non-drinking habits were at greatest risk and exercise was a good way of distracting his desire to get hammered. He hit the gym hard, aware that the few days so far at Nebus had involved sitting about, good food and not much else. He felt stale and didn't want to start looking it too. Weights followed by a session on the exercise bike and then a serious battle with the cross trainer started to get him feeling positive and healthy again and reduced the strong urge to go straight to The Space and put a heavy drinking session onto the Nebus, bill.

After 90 minutes or so he knew sobriety had won again and he had a quick shower and headed for the pool. By then he had expended energy and anger in equal measure and wanted to simply cruise up and down the pool for a while, killing time till a suitable moment for dinner, whilst waiting for Charlotte from bloody Carshalton. After a few lengths of the pool he got bored and felt a little drained. He toweled himself and headed into the sauna to sweat a bit before a strong possibility of a nap before eating.

After a few minutes the door to the sauna opened and a woman in her late 20s came in and sat down on the bench opposite him.

"Bad day at the office?" she suddenly asked out of the blue.

Frank had hardly noticed her as she came in and had not noticed her at all in the gym. He must be slipping, he told himself, as she had a rather tidy figure. No Miss World he thought but if he could still pull anyone who was under 30 he obviously hadn't lost his touch.

"Don't ask," he replied with a smile which suggested charm was set to stun if it could.

"I thought so," the girl continued. "Looked like you wanted to kill someone the way you were battering the weights in there."

"Just taking out a bit of frustration after a bad day," Frank said thinking all the time that he had to come through to Edinburgh more often in the future.

"There is nothing, and I mean nothing worse than being frustrated," said the girl staring straight into Frank's eyes.

Not one for small talk he thought and asked her something about checking how the decor in his room compared to hers.

She smiled and said, "Room number 27. I'm going there now if you would like to have a look around."

"Don't mind if I do," replied Frank and they headed off to compare notes on decor together in the comfort of her room, after the briefest of showers in the changing facilities and wearing the minimum of their clothing.

The young man at reception, who didn't miss much, smiled a hello at Frank and quickly assessed the situation as the young lady who had caught his eye when checking in earlier followed on behind at a trot trying not to look as if they were together.

"Lucky bastard," he whispered under his breath.

The rest of the evening was one Frank would remember forever given half a chance and also one he could boast about to his Para chums, he thought, when he met them next. It would also have a made a good Ealing comedy or Whitehall farce. Jennifer turned out to be there for one night only with a very early start the next day to catch a flight which would ultimately end up with a year in South Africa as a nanny. After ten boring years working for the local council and staying at home with her parents she had embarked on a quest for adventure. After a seriously restricted social life she had started with a fairly wild send off with her friends for a few days in Dundee and had just about recovered enough at the hotel in Edinburgh to consider a final fling with an older man. An older man who was obviously still quite fit. Either way she had no intention of staying in touch or seeing him again even if it broke his heart. Frank's heart was made of sterner stuff and he jumped at the chance to inject a bit of adventure into this young lady's life.

After an exhausting session in her room they caught their breath and ordered food from room service. A platter of sandwiches and salad arrived which they devoured quickly. Refreshed, they made love again in the shower of the room and ended up lying on the bed side by side.

It had been good fun for all concerned but they both knew it was only ever going to be that and an embarrassed silence descended on the room as each waited for the other to make an excuse for going their separate ways. Before Frank could summon up the courage Jennifer surprised him by saying, "I don't want to kick you out or anything but I have a really early start tomorrow and could use a good night's sleep."

Both surprised and relieved Frank nodded, got dressed and, giving her a kiss on the cheek left, promising to keep in touch etc, etc.

He arrived at his room and checked the time. Nine o'clock. Time for a quick shower and then maybe off to bed. He had pretty much written Charlotte off by then but decided a nap was the best course of action whatever lay ahead. His head hit the pillow at 9.20 and he must have been asleep five seconds later. A deep sleep. A very deep sleep where he dreamt of computers, women and club sandwiches in equal measure. The computers were buzzing and flashing and then knocking. Gently at first but slowly and surely getting louder.

Frank woke up to find there was a real knocking coming from his room door and the time was 10.45 pm. He dragged his body out of bed reluctantly, still too drowsy to think clearly. He opened it without saying anything and Charlotte rushed him with her hand grabbing his crotch as they twirled towards his bed. Not only had he been caught off-guard but he had already spent a busy hour or two earlier with young Jennifer and was struggling to rise to the challenge of satisfying Charlotte from Carshalton too. To make this worse, but at least buy him some recovery time, Dr Bernie decided to phone him five minutes after Charlotte arrived in his room.

Citing business talk he excused himself to the bathroom of his room to take that call which he struggled to keep brief. Bernadette had been bored in her flat and, unable to sleep thought she would phone Frank to continue the chat from where it had left off in the canteen. Apologising for the lateness of the hour and finding that by then Frank was also wide awake, she had hoped for a long chat. Frank seemed strangely reluctant to get into any detail regarding any subject she raised and eventually admitted he was quite nervous about the next day's activities and had to try to get some sleep. Bernadette was disappointed but seemed pleased he had been able to admit his nervousness to her. Maybe he had a shy sensitive side after all she mused.

Back in the bedroom Frank put the phone down and jumped back into bed beside Charlotte.

"Who was that?" she asked with a hint of suspicion in her voice.

"That was Dr MacGuiness from Nebus," he emphasised the Dr and Nebus bits as he spoke. "There's a slight change to the plans for tomorrow so I need different stuff with me."

"Kind of late for a phone call like that isn't it," continued Charlotte.

"These boffins work half the night and never pay attention to the time. But to be honest, on the money they are paying me they could phone me at my mother's funeral and I would listen politely."

This seemed to satisfy Charlotte's curiosity and she refrained from asking any more questions as Frank grabbed her under the covers and pulled her towards him.

"Phew, that was close," thought Frank.

Another awkward moment occurred the next morning when Frank came down to breakfast with Charlotte. Jennifer was in the process of checking out at reception when they walked in to view. Frank had smiled at her as casually as he could, taking a step in front of Charlotte to indicate they were not together. Fortunately for Frank Jennifer had started to feel quite embarrassed about her fling with such an older man and after briefly returning is smile turned to reception praying he wouldn't try and stop to talk to her. Frank didn't.

Frank and Charlotte had a long relaxed breakfast. She had finished her training course the day before and only had the journey South to achieve that day, with her shuttle flight booked for 11 in the morning. Frank knew his transport would arrive around nine to collect him and he was ready to go when it did, so they could both relax and make small talk.

Charlotte steered the conversation round to explore the possibilities of keeping in touch. At first the alarm bells went off in Frank's head but when he thought about it he decided it might not be too bad a thing to be able to visit Charlotte in the future. No regular set up of course but a visit to London every now and then could be interesting.

"I tend to be pretty busy most of the time," he started. "But I'll give you my email address and you send me yours. That way we can maybe meet up if we both have time off."

This seemed to be as much as Charlotte had been hoping for and she pocketed the serviette with Frank's email address on it.

A soft voice came over the tanoy informing Mr Chisholm that his transport had arrived. He shrugged his shoulders with a resigned look on his face and, giving her a quick kiss on the lips said, "Duty calls. Remember to send me your email address," and off he went.

Jim was waiting at reception and he joined Frank when he appeared and headed for the car. The usual conversation followed with banter back and forward slighting each other's football allegiances until they arrived once more at Nebus. With a final swipe at Heart of Midlothian FC Frank got out of the MPV and headed into the building. Jim had not been quick enough to come up with a reposte but just laughed briefly and grabbed a thriller from the luggage compartment beside his leg.

Chapter Twelve

Waiting for him in Edinburgh, Delores had got bored quite quickly. She was used to busy days. In fact she was used to everyday being too busy as a rule. A day with no work or responsibilities was far harder to cope with. She had initially tried to set a routine which involved her usual early start. Coffee only, followed by a jog and speed walk was the norm but she didn't want to risk going out in a strange city alone. Instead she started her day by watching a news channel, a luxury she had not enjoyed for a very long time. This crystalized into specifically watching the BBC news channel which she discovered had no adverts on it and was staffed by people who actually seemed to know what they were talking about. After an hour or so of this and a healthy cereal breakfast she would go out for a walk, growing in confidence each day in her new surroundings, as people she had never seen before would say hello in passing or after seeing her out and about perhaps only once. Compared to the car-travel-only set up of her home town, this was very refreshing.

Edinburgh had plenty of hills and steep streets, especially around the area of Edinburgh castle. As she explored the city she would set a brisk pace up these streets to get her breathing going. She also visited the gym each day during the ladies only sessions and began to enjoy the freedom of having time on her hands which she could herself choose how to fill. There were museums and art galleries everywhere and she started to visit them too. History seemed to be dripping off every building here. It oozed from every pore of the old stones which they were made of. There was nothing in her home town as old as the building where her flat was and it was in the New Town of Edinburgh. She found it all a liberating experience. Most of all though, it gave her time to think.

After three days in the flat, she had been collected by car and driven out of Edinburgh to The Nebus Bioscience building. There she had met with Dan's nephew Bobby. He had explained again how ill Blaine had been but had sounded very positive about the chances of his experimental treatment giving him a new lease of life. He was very short on detail and like his uncle, emphasised how sensitive the process was, requiring her to keep anything she learnt to herself. Again without much detail he explained that there would be some changes in Blaine that she would have to get used to but that they would have a better idea of the extent of that after the operation had been completed. She nodded without fully understanding all of what he said but it was clear that was in part, his plan. All she wanted to know was that Blaine would have a chance of surviving and he seemed very confident on this point. As a result she let the rest of what he said wash over her to a large extent.

Bobby gave her a tour of the plant, including part of what he described as the most sensitive area of research where Blaine would come for treatment. When he did, Blaine would need her support. He would have to stay in the plant and she would travel daily from her flat in Edinburgh. There might be times when she could remain with him but the priority was preparing Blaine for the medical procedure. She nodded and was genuinely impressed with the sophistication of the facility. "Money no object," she thought. Dan certainly hadn't scrimped with this place.

By the end of her visit she felt considerably reassured. Bobby had asked if everything was okay with her accommodation and whether she was bored or not. She had enthused sufficiently about the delights and history of Edinburgh to put his mind at rest.

As she shook his hand before leaving he held it for a second and said: "The Blaine you know will come out of the other side fine but you will both have to adapt and work closely together for him to make a full recovery and return to work. You have to commit to this body and soul."

He looked at her with a penetrating stare and she realised it was a question.

"Whatever is necessary," she said, "you can count on me."

She had no idea exactly what that might require but she meant what she said as she said it.

Back at the flat she felt both reassured by her visit and unsettled at the same time if that was possible. The facility was as good as anything she could imagine and she knew that Dan and Bobby would provide whatever was needed to help Blaine, with no limit on cost. The staff she had met she knew would be the best in their fields. None of that worried her. It was just that... There was something intangible about what lay ahead. As if there was something that Bobby and maybe Dan too, weren't telling her. If they knew something that she didn't there was a strong chance that Blaine was aware of it too but had chosen not to confide in her. If that was the case then she had to be concerned. None of them had ever gone into detail about the procedures which were planned to give Blaine a chance of living. She had vaguely thought along the lines of advanced or targeted Chemotherapy but had never dwelt on the details. Maybe it was a magic pill, bone marrow transplant or some new form of radiation. In a way she didn't care as long as it worked and Blaine was saved but the fact that nobody had confided in her what was actually involved, not even Blaine, was starting to annoy her.

Whatever was planned she could do nothing about it except keep her promise to support Blaine in whatever lay ahead. He wouldn't be back for another ten or twelve days at least so for now she had to stay calm and fill her days. The day before her meeting with Bobby she had trawled the internet and all the leaflets in the flat and decided a quiet afternoon of reflection on the thoughts of others each day might be a useful diversion. She had therefore planned a visit to the Scottish Poetry Library just off the Royal Mile where she hoped to rekindle a passion she had enjoyed in her teens, but had shelved in her drive to escape the grinding poverty her parents had endured. Sitting reading Blake or Wordsworth and Tennyson with someone ready to hush any noisy interruptions sounded a good option to take her mind off things. If nothing else it would help fill the days till Blaine came over to Edinburgh for his treatment.

Her days began to take on a structure after that. With the exception of the day she visited Nebus she would fill the days with brisk walks, a museum or gallery every day in the afternoon and enjoy some quiet poetry after her visit to the gym. She became less bored with these diversions but could not stop the growing feeling of anxiety as the date loomed for Blaine to arrive. She badly wanted to see him but at the same time she knew there were huge risks involved and subconsciously wanted to delay the danger as long as possible. Whichever feeling was on the ascendancy, she realised that Edinburgh provided as good a chance of diversions as anywhere she had previously visited.

One day she found herself visiting the National Museum of Scotland in Chamber Street. It was a vast collection of galleries with objects and displays covering every part of the globe and every era in history. Not a whiff of creationism in sight she'd laughed to herself. After a tiring morning touring the first two floors she had gone for lunch in the main cafeteria. At the table next to her was a mother with three young children aged from about five to ten, she guessed. The mother was one of the many who had brought her children here that day out of the rain. The museum was free and had plenty to occupy children of all ages. It represented a low cost but exciting outing for families. The kids all had a cake and a soft drink in front of them and were chatting away excitedly about all the things they had seen and tried out during the visit so far.

After a few minutes the youngest turned to her mother and asked, "When's daddy coming? He promised he would be here."

The mother looked slightly concerned and replied, "He didn't exactly promise. He said he would try to get away from work and join us but he wasn't 100% certain he would make it."

"But he did promise. I heard him say it last night."

There was a bit of toing and froing along these lines with the mother trying to soften the blow if her husband (no doubt as usual) didn't make it to the museum. After ten minutes though, a man of about 40 sneaked up behind the children and with a wink at his wife tapped the children on the shoulders.

They turned round giving Delores a full view of their faces as they lit up.

"It's Daddy," they all shouted in unison. "You're here!"

The man managed somehow to pick up all three of them as they rushed to his arms without hurting or crushing any of them. Delores found that alone an impressive feat.

"I promised I would join you," he said. "I've taken a half day so I am all yours this afternoon. After the museum I thought we could go to the cinema and then have a meal."

The children squealed with joy and kept hugging him. Eventually they let him go and he walked over to his wife and kissed her on the lips.

"Thank you," she mouthed to him. "I love you."

When the kids had finished their cakes and drinks they headed off as a happy family group to explore the delights of the museum together, leaving Delores deep in thought. She had never wanted to be a mother. Not simply because she was ambitious about her career. No, for her, parenthood was the struggle of raising children in poverty and discrimination. Worrying about feeding them every minute of every day. She had watched the worry and stress age and wear down her own parents.

Destroying the days of happiness they should have spent together as a couple and then as a family. They had both died a few years earlier within six months of each other and these struggles had been a huge factor. That was Delores' view of being a child and of raising children. She had come a long way from that and would never risk enduring what her parents had gone through. And yet something in the scene she had just witnessed stayed with her. It hadn't made her broody in any way shape or form. Hell no! But it had made her think of what it must be like for Blaine's wife and children whenever he made it home. It must be better than Christmas for them each time. "It's Daddy" would ring in her ears for the rest of the day she reckoned. Could she really take that away from Blaine's children? Could she be the one who ruined Christmas forever? She shivered a little but knew it wasn't from the cold.

Chapter Thirteen

Frank breezed into Nebus Bioscience, smiled and winked at Fiona as he passed reception and headed straight for the Penicuik Suite. On arrival he noticed everyone was there from the team. He smiled and winked at Bernie as he passed her and made his way to where David was sitting. He made a point of saying hello to everyone by name as he passed them and they all looked up and said hello back. "Oh yes," he thought, "Life is good."

Last night had been great if more than a little tiring. He had avoided an embarrassing moment with Jennifer and had spent a very pleasant breakfast with Charlotte, something he hoped to do every now and again in the future. The banter with Jim on the journey over had been fun. He was sure Fiona was now smiling back at him and knew for a fact that Bernie had returned both his smile and his wink when he had arrived this morning. Life is indeed good.

The plan for the day was to wire Frank up to the remote version of the monitor equipment and test it out with a series of basic movements. Once that had been achieved he would spend most days wearing it while going through a programme of tests and generally going about his daily life. He would have to spend several nights sleeping in the plant to monitor his brain activity whilst resting but nothing else in the way of a challenge lay ahead for the rest of his stay there. The main difficulty he faced that day was staying awake whenever he sat down or lay down while the team adjusted the set up. It even got to the point that David had quietly asked if he needed anything to help him get enough sleep at the hotel.

Frank promised to get a good night's rest before the following day's activities and then remembered his possible dinner date with Bernie. As it turned out they had to quietly agree a rain-check on that as David wanted everyone to work into the evening on the early results so that they could maximise the progress the following day.

Frank looked as disappointed as he could whilst rearranging things with Bernie but was secretly relieved to be able to look forward to an early night. At 3.30 David and the team agreed that they had enough data to work on and Frank could head back to the hotel whenever he liked. He wished them all good luck and headed up to the canteen. Despite his fatigue from recent nocturnal activities he still hoped to see the American beauty again. He was out of luck though and, when the catering assistant brought him the Pasta Carbonara he had ordered, he ate alone. The chef had again excelled himself Frank had to admit. He loitered in the canteen for a while but nobody else appeared and eventually he called it a day and headed off to Jim's waiting MPV.

After the usual banter on the journey back, Frank thanked Jim for the lift even though it was his job to drive him back and forward and headed in to the hotel. The young man on duty at reception looked up at Frank and shook his head signifying no messages that day. Frank gave him the thumbs up and went straight to his room and lay down on the bed. He dosed for about an hour or so then showered, dressed and went for an early meal without giving a thought to the gym or pool. Afterwards he went back to his room, watched part of a documentary about red squirrels and hit the sack before he could fall asleep in the chair.

He slept the sleep of the dead and was still drowsy when the alarm woke him at seven the next morning. As the room-brewed coffee revived him he felt better and more energised than he had for days but then it had been a busy spell he thought. He ate a leisurely breakfast alone and was waiting in the lobby of the hotel when Jim arrived at 8.30 to drive him to Nebus. The day followed a similar pattern to the day before except Frank managed to stay awake throughout the testing and recording sessions.

During a break from specific tests but still wearing the portable scanner on his head and with the pack on his back he took a walk round the different desks where the members of the team were working. He had intended to slowly gravitate to Bernie's desk but she left soon afterwards for her own office. At David's desk his attention was caught by a coloured display on the screen.

It was a rectangular box with most of the space displayed as red. In amongst the red were a few isolated dots of green.

David looked round and saw Frank scanning the computer screen.

"This represents the entirety of your brain activity," he began. "The green dots are the parts which we have recorded and stored so far. Over the next two weeks we have to turn all the red areas green by recording every possible function within your brain. It's a rather simplified representation, however, it is useful for the team to keep a track of progress to date. Any areas which are currently red are thrown up in far more detail on Jon and Bernie's computers so that we can keep covering new ground but it will give you an idea of where we are at."

"When it all turns green I can go home?" asked Frank.

"Essentially that's right. We will need to double check every area has been recorded afterwards but hopefully that will only take a day or two. If we need to redo anything it's easier if you are still here. Incidentally, Bobby is running an identical scan on one of their American test subjects as part of the work being done in D Section. With a bit of luck we can compare notes as a precursor to recording more subjects here. Either way he has insisted on a complete recording of your brain function to the standards they use there, so we have to get it spot on. It's also important that you don't meet their test subject during the recording process apparently, though I can't think how it would affect anything we are recording."

"Their subject isn't a gorgeous black woman in her mid-thirties by any chance?" asked Frank.

"No, some business guy roughly ages with yourself," Replied David absently. "Bobby said that was why you were selected. They needed to compare like with like for the work they are doing and it seems you and their Yank were a match in that respect. It wouldn't matter so much for our purposes here. Anyone would have done."

David quickly added: "Although we are very pleased with your help and co-operation."

He looked round to make sure he hadn't offended Frank and was relieved to see he hadn't before adding: "I take it you slept better last night?"

"Yes, much better thanks."

Frank was staring at the screen when all of sudden a few more areas turned green.

David noticed the surprise on Frank's face.

"Bernie must have verified what we did this afternoon and uploaded it to the computer in the States. All your details are stored there so that D Section can confer with their associated departments over there. Not ideal from our point of view but we need to use some pretty big computers and we simply don't have access to them in this country yet."

Frank seemed fascinated by his graph. To be honest, he had never credited his brain as being so interesting till now or realised how big a computer would be needed to store its functions. He took it all as a compliment somehow. "I must be brighter than I thought," he thought to himself and watched to see if this realisation fired up some more green areas on the screen. He was disappointed to note that it didn't.

After some further bending stretching and lifting he was dismissed for the day and headed for the canteen again. He knew in advance that all the members of his team were fully engaged in assessing his massive brain power but again hoped to see the American woman of his dreams. Again he was disappointed. He ate the smoked salmon and scrambled egg he had ordered when it arrived and after loitering again over his glass of fruit juice headed back to the hotel once more.

He was still full of energy from his unusually good night's sleep and immediately changed in his room ready for the gym. After a vigorous workout he swam lengths of the small pool for 30 minutes and headed for the sauna. "Will luck be a lady again tonight he wondered," checking the door every now and again hoping to make yet another new acquaintance in the sweltering heat.

After 20 minutes or so the door of the sauna opened and two very overweight businessmen came in. They nodded at him and continued their previous conversation in German. One of them was obviously German but the other spoke the language more slowly and hesitantly with a hint of a Scottish accent peeping through every now and again.

Frank had a thing about fat people and left before his appetite could be ruined. He showered and dressed then headed back to his room. The night was yet young he decided and spruced himself up for dinner. With his recent luck, he was bound to find some lonely lady in "The Space" who would welcome his company and join him to eat or for drinks afterwards.

As he arrived at the restaurant though and looked around he was disappointed. A few couples, groups and pairs of business men but no single women. Even the serving staff were all guys that night although one of them seemed particularly keen to please Frank. The night being a write-off was confirmed when the two fat German speakers arrived and sat at the next table.

The bar area proved as barren an area as the leisure centre and dining area had been and after more glasses of fresh orange than Frank could actually enjoy he headed for his room. When he phoned her, Bernie was busy again with his records and doubted whether she would have much free time while they were still at the recording phase.

Frank channel hopped on his TV for a while before settling on a war film. Steve McQueen as a Psychotic bomber pilot competing with Robert Wagner for the affections of the film's love interest seemed to be the gist of it. Frank was something of a Steve McQueen fan but hadn't seen this old black and white film before. He had watched "The Great Escape" and the "Magnificent Seven" two dozen times each, always seeing himself as McQueen but this was a new one. As McQueen refused to bail out of the stricken aircraft at the end and smashed into the white cliffs of Dover, he felt let down and vowed not to watch it again.

Although not really tired he brushed his teeth, put on his new pajamas for the first time and got into bed. Sleep came slowly and in fits. He had to admit he had felt a bit deflated when David had told him he was there as a match for some yank rather than because of his supreme fitness and abilities in the gym. He didn't entirely understand why it made a difference but it did. Each time he closed his eyes though, he saw the box with the red and green areas and found it somehow disturbing, as if his personality was being taken away from him one piece at a time and shared with strangers who didn't appreciate him.

Chapter Fourteen

Two days later Delores was dressed to impress and stood in Edinburgh airport with Bobby and another of his doctors waiting for Blaine to arrive. She desperately wanted to see him and spend time with him but the doubts about splitting up his family had remained with her from the day at the museum.

Eventually Blaine and Vic Zelnik appeared through the arrivals gate. Blaine looked a bit pale but not really any worse than when she had last seen him. If anything he looked slightly better rested. Maybe time with his family had helped him. She walked over and gave him a brief hug, still not fully comfortable with public displays of affection. Blaine gave her a squeeze round her waist and sneaked a brief kiss on her cheek.

"I've missed you," he whispered in her ear.

"Me too," she whispered back.

Together they walked out of the building to the pickup/ drop off point where a company people carrier was waiting. The driver put down the paperback he was reading and got out to help them with their luggage. Once everyone was safely on board he drove smoothly out of the airport towards the Edinburgh bypass.

Nobody spoke during the journey. Delores and Blaine sat next to each other and held hands. Bobby Bartleman and Vic Zelnik sat together but didn't speak. Bobby's medical colleague sat in the passenger seat beside the driver and looked out of the window. He didn't like Scotland, didn't like Edinburgh and didn't much like the work he did for Nebus, but it paid very well.

The driver didn't mind any of them but had long since learned to gauge the mood of his passengers and only engage in conversation when they wanted to. On this trip the mood was not chatty so he focused on the task of driving and nothing else. He and his colleague Jim took it in turn to provide whatever transport was necessary and only met when two vehicles were needed. On these few occasions they would compare notes on recent journeys and swap a large pile of paperback thrillers to while away the long gaps between driving duties. He wondered if Jim had had such a quiet group before and planned to ask him next time they met up.

When they arrived at Nebus, they all got out except Vic Zelnik who was booked into a hotel for the night and then had a seat booked taking him straight back to the states. Blaine had made it here safe and sound so he had done his part. Whatever lay ahead was in the hands of Dr Bobby Bartleman and his team at Nebus Bioscience. To be honest that suited Old Vic fine. He didn't like travel and was exhausted by the recent flurry of flights and extra duties he had had to undertake. He couldn't wait to get back home and into the old routine at Nebus head office which consisted of not very much work and long lunch breaks in between.

The others made their way into the building with the duty driver bringing along the luggage on a specially provided trolley. There, an American gorilla of a guard called Nick took charge of the trolley. Where do they get them from, the driver wondered, and headed back to the people carrier for the short journey to Dr Zelnik's hotel near the airport. After that he was finished for the evening and could head off home. Jim had the morning trip to the airport on his schedule and not much else. A collect at The Hilton near the airport, a drop off from Nebus to a serviced flat in Edinburgh's New Town followed by about 150 pages of a paperback before taking the Hilton passenger back. No wonder they had both put on weight doing this job.

Inside the plant the small group of new arrivals followed Nick to D Section and made their way inside to an accommodation suite which backed on to The Nebraska Suite. Seeing the name Blaine briefly thought of his wife and family back home but quickly dismissed the image from his mind, though he did find the name comforting somehow.

The accommodation was spotless and looked very comfortable. Bobby explained that Blaine would have to remain in D Section for about two weeks but after that, all being well, he could move to a more relaxing venue to recuperate with Delores. Timings would depend on progress with the process of medical examinations and the treatment itself. Meanwhile there would be food available at all times and anything else he required could be arranged. Bobby would be about during daytime hours and Nick at night time should Blaine need anything.

"You'll probably find yourself quite tired by the end of each session and have to sleep," Bobby said at the end of his briefing. Then he added without realising the irony: "Delores will be accommodated in Edinburgh in the evenings. Tonight though we thought you might both like to spend the night here. There's an excellent Scottish chef here who enjoys producing great meals and I've asked him to stay on tonight and cook up something special. It will be served here in the Apartment at 7.30. I'll see you tomorrow."

And with that Bobby, his colleague and Nick left Blaine and Delores alone. After the obligatory long hug and passionate kiss they sat together on the sofa, conscious that dinner would be served there quite soon. Despite everything they had shared there was now an awkwardness about being together. Both were nervous about what the future held and the dangers of the medical treatment which lay ahead but there was more to it than that.

Blaine knew the details of what he faced and wished he could tell Delores everything. That, however, would have been difficult. How do you tell someone you love that your only hope of being with them was essentially to become somebody else and expect them to understand? He felt guilty about not sharing this aspect of the plan with Delores and he could tell that she knew he was keeping something to himself and that she resented it.

Delores did indeed feel left out of the situation but was prepared to accept that on trust. Maybe it was habit. Even as Blaine's PA she was regularly kept out of some of the most sensitive business meetings where new plans with the potential to greatly change share prices and profits were discussed. But there was more to her unease than just that. She had expected Blaine to arrive looking more ill than when she had seen him last, paler and fading away. Instead, after two weeks at home with Beth and the children he had returned looking so much healthier. Still obviously ill, but more rested and relaxed. She still had the vision of the family at the museum in her head and couldn't shake it. A voice deep within her brain kept asking, "Can you really steal a husband and father."

Dinner arrived and they ate it together at the table. It was a delicious meal of Coquilles St Jacques in a ginger dressing, Chateau Briand following by something called Cranachan which neither had even heard of before. As they ate they talked and began to laugh and relax. Both were determined to put the other at their ease and

141

although the laughter was forced and false at first they slowly returned to a familiar mood of enjoying each other's company.

After they had finished eating, Delores pushed the trolley out of the apartment into the corridor and locked the door. Blaine had followed her and held her tightly as she turned back from the door. They made love in the king size bed which had been conveniently provided for the purpose, but it was a mere physical act. Both were lost in their own thoughts throughout.

Afterwards Blaine fell asleep immediately, exhausted from the travel and his illness but Delores lay awake for hours finding it impossible to sleep.

"Can you really steal and husband and a father?" she kept hearing.

In the morning they both rose early and dressed long before any of the staff might arrive. It was strange but old habits, even now when everyone here knew about them, died hard.

They had arranged to meet Bobby in his office which was close to the Nebraska Suite at 9.30, after having breakfast in the apartment. Blaine was due to go through a medical to check his general health and was then going to be connected to some monitoring computers which would have to be calibrated accurately for the early part of his treatment. As a result it had been agreed that

Delores would head off back to her serviced flat in Edinburgh and return to have dinner with Blaine that evening. In fact that would form the pattern for much of the next two weeks she had been told. Again this had made her feel excluded and for the first time just a little resentful. After breakfast she kissed Blaine quickly on the cheek and headed off to the waiting transport.

Blaine headed to Bobby's office almost relieved that Delores was away and would be for much of the time he was here. He was finding it stifling to spend time with her without being able to be completely honest. He was also starting to doubt that she would go along with the whole plan when she discovered the full details. It was a big ask of anyone.

But there was also something else at the back of his mind. During the two weeks he had spent at home he had got over the usual feeling of claustrophobia remarkably quickly. Admittedly he had been waited on hand and foot by Beth and spoiled with hugs and kisses by his kids. Anyone would have appreciated that, he knew. For the first time in a long while he had actually enjoyed spending time with his wife and family. The holidays camping in the national parks had been fun but mainly because he had enjoyed the peace and tranquillity of camping in the National parks. His family, he realised on reflection, had actually been detracting from the experience. But at home this time it had been different. He had felt a peacefulness that had been absent from his life for a very long time and he knew that his health had improved slightly as a result. He had even managed to play soccer with young Daniel one day. Not for long but the hour or so represented a first and he had genuinely enjoyed the whole idea. He knew he was wavering and waited for his inner voice to tell him to "stick with the plan" but it didn't come.

Chapter Fifteen

The next day Frank awoke tired again but this time for no good reason. A quick dip in the pool failed to revive him and he sat in relative silence with Jim on the journey to the Nebus facility. With no real enthusiasm he headed inside resigned to a mundane day as a performing guinea pig for the team of child prodigies studying him.

The next week followed a similar pattern with constant testing, recording and early returns to a hotel he now found boring and mundane. The novelty of being pampered had worn off and he had started to count the days till he could go home and get back to the old routine. He phoned Paddy a few times and even Charlotte after she sent her phone number to him in her email.

His luck with the ladies seemed to have deserted him and despite daily forays to the leisure complex and the bar he had no further takers for his company. Each day he studied the graph on the computer to see how much of it had turned green and how much remained red. Part of him wanted it all to go green so that he could go home but another part of him seemed more and more disturbed as each section of the graph changed colour. He did not know why. But it did.

Although the name had been mentioned often enough to make him seem part of the team, Dr Robert "Bobby" Bartleman did not actually put in an appearance while Frank was there until the start of the third and final week. He appeared unannounced, while Frank was being recorded playing chess, a game he had only a rudimentary understanding of. Bobby had been in the Penicuik suite for some time before Frank saw him and his surprise at seeing a stranger there was probably sufficient to turn a whole lot of the graph from red to green.

Bobby walked over to Frank and introduced himself in a very measured and educated American accent. They shook hands, with Frank careful not to hurt the hand which was likely to be signing his paycheck.

"Sorry we haven't managed to meet before now but things have been a bit hectic. I gather the team are making great progress with their scanning and recording. I hope you have been looked after. Is the hotel okay for you?"

Frank was about to make a quip about the recent lack of single women at the Hilton of late but decided against it.

"Yes, very comfortable thanks. No problems at all."

"Food okay?" Bobby continued with his polite interest in Frank's well-being.

"Very good thanks, especially here in your canteen. I have no complaints at all."

"Good, good," said Bobby. "I believe David has mentioned that we have a matching project underway in D Section. It may be necessary to get you in there for a session before you leave us. Any objections?"

Frank's mind immediately raced to visions of the American lady he had seen in the canteen.

"None. None at all," he said with genuine enthusiasm. "I'd be delighted."

"Good, good," said Bobby again with a strange hint of anxiety in his voice. "I'll keep you posted and arrange a time later this week. For now we both better get back to the task in hand."

Frank nodded and smiled before reluctantly returning to the chess board. After chess he played snakes and ladders, poker for real money online, table tennis and watched Jeremy Kyle on daytime TV. He reluctantly smoked a cigarette, drank some beer and generally was forced to carry out a whole range of tasks to record his reactions. Over the course of the last five days he had been put into all sorts of possible situations and his brain function recorded. David had deliberately started an argument and tried to needle him about his army service, his drinking, his ex-wives and his kids. "You're a brave little bastard," Frank had thought at the time as a genuine desire to punch David's lights out had flashed through his mind.

All the time this was going on the team were recording and checking the data. Each day when he arrived Frank would have a look at the graph on David's computer and see more green and less red. By the end of week two there was still a lot of red on the screen. It had been at that point that Frank had had to sleep over at the lab for a few nights. David had explained that they would be inducing certain brain activity as he slept to cover areas not yet recorded.

If Frank was honest about it, he was glad of the change of scene. The hotel was nice enough, he couldn't fault it but after the initial success with the ladies, pickings had been slim and he had become bored there. Bernie had been so busy they had never managed to have dinner together and he was not hopeful this would ever happen. Most of all though he just wanted the testing to stop so that he could go home. He wanted to get back to his daily routine. He wanted to be in charge again, shouting at his boot camp squad in the mornings at the seafront, getting his private clients fitter and getting himself away from kids with brains the size of planets. Here he was a guinea pig getting ordered around and he didn't like it. There was also that nagging sense of being exploited despite the generous amount they were paying him (half of which had already been paid into his bank account) and the posh hotel. Something about that graph bugged him too.

He didn't feel any different in some ways but the graph gave him a weird sense of being stolen bit by bit.

When the activities were over for the day he went up to the canteen for his now customary late lunch and ordered toasted ciabata with artichokes and sun dried tomatoes. Again the chef came up trumps but his appetite just wasn't there. The canteen had a few kids in lab coats but nobody he recognised and yet again the beautiful American apparition never re-appeared.

He ate with little enthusiasm and finished his fresh apple juice before leaving the building, on this occasion, without his usual loitering delay. As ever, Jim was waiting in the car park and as ever put down his paperback thriller as Frank arrived.

Jim sensed Frank was not on top form and drove silently out of the car park. After a few minutes Frank asked: "What do you think of this Nebus mob. Honestly, I'll not go telling tales."

Jim thought for a moment before answering.

"I'll be honest. It's the best job I've had for ages. They pay well. The benefits are good and it's hardly a tough shift. Occasional early starts but the main problem is keeping busy. I read a book every two days during working hours and nobody minds. Everybody else I know working here enjoys it too. My nephew's the chef. Again apart from preparing the meals in the canteen with no real budget control he is under employed most of the time and is studying for a degree in English through the Open University. He has plenty of time between meals. Only gets disturbed when some smart ass orders something difficult. Says there's some bastard doing that at the moment in the afternoons which is upsetting his studies. Probably one of the yanks; they're like that sometimes. But he says he'll give them some of his special sauce if they keep it up and they'll never eat there again."

Frank made a mental note to stick to the menu from now on and maybe eat at a different time for the rest of the remaining week.

"Overall though, they're good to work for. I've never had any problems. If you do your job and show up when you're meant to nobody gives you grief."

Frank just nodded and returned to his own thoughts. Bored and anxious to get home as he was, he knew he was in the home straight now. Just like a long run or a big session in the gym he had to just keep going and not look at the clock. It would all be over soon enough.

Back at the hotel he said goodbye to Jim after arranging a pick up time for the next day and headed for his room. He was bored and knew this was dangerous territory for a reformed alcoholic. After all, he was staying in a Hilton hotel with an American multinational picking up the tab. The bar and restaurant were open all day. Room service

24/7 for residents. The desire for a drink was almost overwhelming. It hadn't helped that the kids had made him take a drink as part of their testing and recording. He knew it was to try to initiate a specific response form him for them to record and turn another little bit of their graph green. This, it had achieved. But it had achieved something else in him too. He desperately wanted a drink. He had only drunk a half pint of beer but it was enough to give him a taste for it again. He now knew how a shark felt when it detected one part in a million of blood in the water. It wanted more blood. Lots of blood. A leg, an arm and all the blood inside them and it wouldn't stop till it had had so much blood that it couldn't possibly manage another thing. Not even a waffer thin mint. Frank needed blood too or at least a bucket full of drink.

He fought it and fought it. Until the half pint of beer at Nebus, he had not touched a drink for the best part of ten years. But they had made him drink it. That smart little shit and all his smart little shitty pals just to see how he would react. That child doctor who had needled him about his wives and marriages and kids. Christ I should have knocked his fucking block off there and then. Well if they wanted him to have a drink and see what happened then he would keep them happy. He would have such a lot to drink at their expense that parts of the graph which didn't even exist would turn green when he was finished. Fuck it! I'm going to get hammered he decided and headed for the bar without having a shower.

Have a plan and stick to it Frank remembered someone telling him once and that night he stuck to his task. He had started by making it crystal clear to the barman that all the drinks were going on the tab for his room. An instruction he started repeating unnecessarily as the night wore on. At first he was good company and a welcome distraction to the business folk booked into the hotel. Then he became a bore they could do without and many of them headed early to their rooms. After that he became a danger to their well-being and finished as an incident number with Lothian and Borders police who were eventually called when the barman refused to serve him any more drink, resident or not. By the time the police arrived though the drink had caught up with him and he was a danger to no one.

A voice at the back of his head kept repeating: "Don't start a fight with the police."

He even said it out loud at one point, much to the relief of the two police officers who arrived to deal with the incident. They had eyed Frank with professional caution when they arrived at first and were very relieved when he sat down, told everyone he loved them all and fell asleep. They took sufficient details to cover their backs and then woke Frank up and help him to his room. He managed to land on his bed already in the recovery position and they left when the night manager promised to ensure his safety through the night.

The next day Jim arrived to collect Frank as arranged and was surprised when he didn't appear. After a while he popped inside to reception where a relieved night manager was waiting for him with a blow by blow account of Frank's antics the night before, albeit no blows had been struck. Jim had instructions to collect Frank each morning and deliver him safely to Nebus Biosciences Scottish Research Facility, a duty he took seriously. As a result he headed up to Frank's room with the daytime manager who was armed with a master key.

They opened the door to the room and looked in. The bed looked like it had been hit by a tsunami but was empty. Taps were running in the bathroom, so the receptionist, by agreement with Jim, headed back to his post. Jim shouted "Hello" and headed into the room.

Frank came out of the bathroom dressed in slacks, a blazer, collar and tie. Or that was Jim's first impression until he realised it was someone about the same size and build as Frank but it wasn't him.

"I'm Paddy," said Paddy in a not unfriendly tone. "Who are you?"

"I'm Jim," said Jim. "I'm here to drive Frank to the Nebus plant."

"He'll be one hour late today. Is that a problem?"

Jim surveyed the room and decided what ever had happened to Frank was serious enough to cause a delay and one hour didn't seem too bad in the circumstances. This guy Paddy sounded like he had it under control and Jim didn't fancy arguing with him anyway.

"Nope," said Jim. "I'll square it with the lab guys. Everyone sleeps in some time or another."

"Cheers mate," said Paddy and returned to the bathroom.

Jim headed for his vehicle, spoke to David advising him that Frank had slept in and was running about an hour or so late and picked up his paperback. David wasn't best pleased but these things happened. They would just have to work Frank a bit later that evening. It was no "biggy".

Jim read on, oblivious to the drama continuing in the hotel as Frank endured his second cold bath and drank the endless glasses of water and coffee Paddy handed him.

Paddy had been wakened the night before from a deep sleep by an incoherent idiot on the other end of the phone. After a minute or two he realised it was Frank and that Frank was as drunk as a skunk. After endless ramblings about how good a mate Paddy was and how they should have gone out in a blaze of glory in their army days, shooting from the hip like Butch and Sundance, Paddy managed to get Frank to give him some clues to his whereabouts.

After a few more minutes of rambling Paddy could picture the scene. Frank had been bored. There were no single women about and someone else was paying for all the drink he could consume. Whoever was paying for the drink was to blame for Frank being bored so fuck them, he'd get pissed. There had been a discussion which had become an altercation and the police had been called. Nobody had actually got hurt, yet, but Frank sounded like he was talking himself into correcting that particular oversight. At his work Paddy dealt with people all the time who were suicidal. It was a fairly easy switch to deal with someone who was homicidal.

After getting Frank to promise not to leave his room till Paddy got there, he'd dressed, explained the situation to Mary and headed out. Mary had been used to Paddy getting called out during the night when he was still in the army and was sleepy enough to accept it for now even though he was a civilian. "Frank needed help, the CO wanted to see him, the boys were fighting downtown, Kuwait had been invaded." Whatever. "Just as long as I can go back to sleep."

Paddy had sorted it all each time (Kuwait, admittedly, with some help) and come back safely to her. This was just another midnight callout.

Paddy drove as swiftly as he could without getting stopped for speeding and made it to the hotel. Luckily some other guests arrived from a late night in town just as he was wondering how to get in without attracting any more attention on what had clearly been a lively night for the staff.

He made his way straight to Frank's room. It had taken him 30 minutes to wake Frank and get him to let him in. What he found wasn't encouraging. The room smelled badly of containing a drunk. The bed clothes were everywhere but on the bed. A glass table top was smashed as was a cup and saucer. Worst of all Frank had immediately fallen unconscious again on top of the broken glass.

Paddy's only gentle action of the night was to carefully lift Frank's slumped body away from the glass and remove three pieces which had stuck to his side. Thereafter he dropped him and left him to sleep it off for a while. The room came next and a fingertip search for all the pieces of glass and shattered pottery. This took a long time but was achieved quietly.

A quick look at his watch after that, showed Paddy the time was now 7 am. Time to get to work on reviving Frank. A cold shower restored some vague signs of life but only just. A cold bath followed which worked better. Then coffee followed by water in the remaining glass.

Frank failed to respond to the words of encouragement from Paddy who then repeated the whole routine. Frank started to show signs of wanting to kill Paddy who took this as a good sign. Another cup of coffee and a violent vomit and Frank could talk English again after a fashion.

Again Paddy decided he was making progress. He also managed to find out that Frank was due to be collected at 8.30. Looking at his watch he knew he would not make it. No problem. He can phone in sick once he was coherent enough or reschedule the transport. For now he had to get the drink out of Frank and avoid anything which would jeopardise his future sobriety or his paycheck from Nebus, in that order. It wouldn't do any harm if Frank could appologise to the hotel staff for his behaviour. The police could be dealt with in due course if necessary. For now though, all Frank could manage was, "fuck off you old bastard," but even that was progress.

By the time Jim arrived Frank was in his third bath which was at least slightly tepid as a reward for being more polite to Paddy. He had eaten and kept down a bacon roll and was now able to say sorry when Paddy hit him. The cuts from the glass were mercifully shallow and had stopped bleeding during the first cold bath. From years of experience, some at least of it personal, Paddy had estimated one hour was needed.

Just 63 minutes after Jim had sat back in his vehicle Frank arrived at the passenger door fully dressed and looking mainly alive. Admittedly he was a lot whiter than usual and not his usual jocular self but Jim was happy enough to have his passenger and to be able to head for the plant. He decided on balance not to talk about football that day.

Chapter Sixteen

Bobby shook hands with Blaine as he entered his office and motioned for him to sit down. He looked him up and down in a professional way and said, "You seem to be dealing with things very well so far. How do you feel?"

"I feel better for the rest at home," replied Blaine honestly. "I still get tired and still have the pains where you'd expect but overall I'm not too bad."

"Good," said Bobby. "The better your health at this stage the better all round. As we both know that won't last for ever and we need to move quickly with the next stage. In simply terms we need to record a full map of your brain's activity, in every possible situation. We need to do the same for movement and memory. This takes time but we have developed methods to do much of this while you sleep. Once we have a full record and have checked it thoroughly we will be ready to go."

"Talk me through this word 'go' in detail please," said Blaine with his eyes straight on Bobby's face.

"Okay. Once we have a complete record of you and a complete record of the donor we lie you both down, wire you up and stop the brain for a split second. We start it up again but feed your records to the donor and his into you. The result is both waking up conscious and aware as before but having swapped bodies. It's as simple as that."

To Blaine, it suddenly didn't sound that simple and doubt was again flooding into his thoughts.

Bobby could see it and continued: "This will be the fifth time we have carried out the procedure and all the others were successful. I won't claim it is routine: It is not. It is a revolutionary method of prolonging life but we can do this and for you it is the only option available."

"And for the other poor son-of-a-bitch?"

"He has been well compensated and is convinced he can beat the cancer. Either way he is up and running with the recording of his brain activity and is raring to go. He would be upset if anything got in his way now."

Bobby waited to gauge Blaine's reaction. After a pause Blaine nodded and said: "Well then, what are we waiting for?" with what he hoped was more conviction than he felt inside.

After that Blaine felt as if he had lit the blue touch paper on a firework but forgotten to stand back. He was whisked round D Section in a blur of activity. Medicals, questionnaires, fittings for equipment to get wired to, what seemed like, every bit of him and no time for lunch. Not that he noticed. It was an impressive set up and was full of people who seemed to know exactly what they were doing.

The day disappeared in a flash until he found himself back at the apartment exhausted. Delores was there waiting for him and he longed to bring her in on the secrets of what lay ahead but knew he could not. Not yet. That would have to wait till everything was done and she could see for herself what had happened. If anything went wrong the plan was still to leave her and Beth in complete ignorance of what he had tried.

Delores could see he was exhausted and decided to spoil him a bit. He looked like he needed it tonight. She ran him a nice hot bath and poured a selection of essential oils into it that she bought for that specific purpose. She undressed him and helped him into the water then bathed him like a child eventually stripping and joining him in the water. They stayed there till the water started to cool, soaping each other down and giggling like kids. She got out first, quickly dried herself and again helped him out. His movements were laboured as he climbed out of the bath; partly from his illness but mainly she realised from fatigue. This whole thing was draining him.

Dinner arrived and they ate together. Unlike the evening before they didn't talk much, both lost in their own thoughts. Afterwards Delores took his arm and walked him to the bed.

To save him any embarrassment she said, "No excitement tonight for you. Doctors' orders. You get a good night's sleep and I'll see you back here tomorrow evening."

They kissed each other full on the lips but not in the usual lingering way and Blaine crawled gratefully into the bed alone. Delores pulled the covers up to his chin and tucked him in. He was asleep before she had even collected her coat and handbag.

The next day started earlier for Blaine but he had slept well and took a vague interest in the recording equipment to which he was wired up. The day passed as he carried out a selection of basic tasks while standing, sitting, walking or lying down. Nothing too taxing he thought, suspecting that wouldn't last, but for now, being politely ordered around suited him. It was distraction enough from all the conflicting thoughts rushing around in his head. He wondered if the machinery could record them or even make sense of them for him and laughed.

Bobby was there throughout the days of testing and recording. All his American staff seemed to know what they were doing but nobody seemed as confident or knowledgeable in Blaine's eyes as Bobby. He would stand beside staff members and question them or advise day in day out. A tweak of a dial here, a twist of a knob there; he understood it all. He also took time to explain much of what was going on to Blaine, reassuring him after each session and showing him a graph of red areas which he explained summarised what had still to be mapped and recorded.

"When all of that is green," he explained to Blaine, "and we've triple checked it, we'll be ready to go."

Blaine found himself at the start and at the end of each day studying the graph carefully for progress. He knew he was exhausted easily these days and the pain he felt in his stomach and neck appeared to be getting slightly more noticeable. But something else was slowly gripping him as the days went by. It was excitement. No other word for it. He found the whole prospect exciting. Doing nothing meant dying young he knew, so in that sense this course of action had been forced upon him, but to have the chance to be at the forefront of scientific advancement was exciting.

The childish enthusiasm of it surprised him as it overtook the feelings of fear. He was part of a team making history here. The fact that it would also save his life was good and getting a super fit body to replace his own dying carcass was a bonus too. All that though, was secondary to being part of a group which was close to playing god. Bobby had explained they were upping the pain killing drugs which he had to take and there might be some delusionary side-lines, dizziness and nausea. Blaine hadn't paid much attention and didn't necessarily factor that in to his new feelings. He knew that he felt good about what was going to happen, all of a sudden though.

Chapter Seventeen

The day was one of the longest Frank could remember. David and his team had a lot planned for the day and they were none too happy at the delay. David was about to criticise Frank as he arrived but took one look at the expression on his face and thought better of it.

Co-ordination was Frank's initial problem over and above his mood, pallor and dry mouth. A number of tasks had to be repeated and the readings they were getting on the computers at first were largely unusable. Polite requests to repeat actions seemed unwelcome and when they wired Frank up for a test carried out whilst lying down he fell asleep and was difficult to waken.

As the day wore on, however, Frank became a better subject and some of his old humour returned. He swore less and was able to get most tasks right first time. David cheered up too and his team made best use of what data they could get, filling in more of their graphs with green instead of red.

Bernie seemed particularly unimpressed with Frank and he guessed that he had blown any chance there and also that it was obvious to all concerned that he had been on the bender of a lifetime which might jeorpardise all their work. Most of all Frank just wanted to get back to his hotel room and sleep.

Eventually his wish was granted and he was dismissed for the day. As it was later than usual he gave the canteen a miss and headed for Jim's transportation service. Jim looked at Frank and gauged that he was in a better state than he had been that morning.

"Big night," he inquired cautiously.

"The biggest for a while," said Frank, prepared at least to make small talk. "Just don't mention football."

Jim took the advice and kept the banter safe and low key. The journey took longer than usual as they hit the rush hour traffic which did Frank's hangover no good whatsoever. After what appeared to be a lifetime and after one stop for Frank to throw up they made it to the hotel. Jim bid Frank a cheery goodbye and headed off. Frank went straight to his room and collapsed on the bed.

The next day was a day of apologies for Frank, starting of course with Paddy. Frank had only a vague recollection of Paddy arriving but knew he had worked enough magic to save the contract and Frank's blushes. The hotel staff came next followed by the team at Nebus. A visit to Doc Gibson had been arranged to check that the drinking session had had no long term effects on Frank's health or the accuracy of the programme. Bernie had calmed down but not enough to take up the offer of a date anytime soon.

By the end of the day Frank felt sufficiently redeemed to have returned to his usual optimistic self as he returned to the hotel. The following day would be his last at Nebus if all went well and the red had all turned to Green. There wasn't much red to go and everyone had seemed pleased with the overall progress made to date. Even Dr Bobby had put in an appearance in the late afternoon to praise everyone's efforts. He had taken Frank aside and in a friendly and conspiratory way had advised a visit to D Section was planned for the following evening. He had said it such a way that it sounded like a reward. If section D built women like the American model he had seen then maybe it would be worth a visit.

Either way Frank was in the home straight. Half the fee had already been paid into his account, the other half had been promised the Monday after he finished. Nebus had even agreed to pay the sundry invoices he had submitted for "clothing purchased". Nobody had mentioned the minor incident at the hotel, or the police or the drinks he had bought for everyone who was in the bar at the start of the night. Drinks added to his room bill. A bill which included some damage to furniture. They were very generous here and fortunately very forgiving. All he had to do now was tidy up some recording the following day and pay a late visit to D Section. All in all, a walk in the park.

He headed back to the hotel that night in fine spirits and returned to his traditional pastime of slagging Hearts Football team to the exasperation of Jim who tried, but did not quite manage to give as good as he got. "Maybe," Frank thought, "that was merely out of politeness to visitors to Nebus." Who cared though, big Frank was heading home soon with enough readies in his bank account to take a very well earned holiday. He could maybe even visit Carshalton on the way there or back. Oh yes he was back on a roll.

He bounced out of bed early the next day and after a quick swim and workout, showered and dressed in a smart but casual blue sweater and slacks set which, he was pleased to think, had now been paid for by Nebus. He felt good. Looking in the mirror he decided he looked good too. One last attempt at impressing Dr Bernie wouldn't hurt. He enjoyed a very full and nutritious breakfast, now safe in the knowledge that its health and energy providing qualities would not be required to sustain him in the gym at Nebus that day or ever again.

Jim arrived bang on time at 8.30 and they headed off around the bypass trading blows against each other's beloved team, knowing that their jousting would soon come to an end and enjoying it all the more for that fact. Frank mentioned as they arrived at the plant that he would be a bit later than usual leaving in the evening. Jim put out a hand to shake Frank's and explained he was finishing early to take his wife to the cinema so this was farewell.

"You're not too bad for a bluenose," he said as they shook hands.

"Pity you're a Jambo bastard," Frank replied and smiled as he headed towards reception.

Jim picked up his paperback, the third that week and started reading.

Inside the team were ready and waiting with smiles all round. David confirmed that only a few gaps remained and they could induce most of the data they required while Frank rested later that day and in the morning they only had a few tests to repeat to check readings and calibrations on stuff already covered. Frank was in too good a mood at the prospect of going home to worry that it might be re-doing some of what had been tested after his lapse at the bar. Everyone seemed happy and an end of term type of atmosphere permeated the Penicuik suite. Frank almost felt sorry he was going to be heading home the next day. Almost. Even Bernie smiled at him again. "I wonder," he thought, before deciding he would be a good boy and hopefully not be kept too late at school that evening.

They all went to lunch together for once and even Doc Gibson and Nurse Mrs Gibson joined them. Frank felt like it was his birthday, a feeling accentuated when a cake arrived from the kitchen after they had all eaten their main course. No candles or piping with his name he noted.

"We asked the chef to produce something special for the last day we would all be together," David explained, looking even more childlike than ever. "The chef here is excellent and loves being given a challenge."

Frank looked for any evidence of "special sauce" from a pissed-off chef but decided he was safe enough and helped himself to a huge slice as it was passed around. It wasn't half bad he thought as he took a large forkful.

After lunch they all headed back to the Penicuik suite and most of the team began number crunching on their computers. The only one who didn't was Bernie who walked over to Frank when everyone else was busy.

"I knew from your records you had been a piss head but I thought you were over it," she said in a remarkably friendly way.

"I was," Frank started, "but I got really bored and lonely in the hotel and decided to get drunk and start a fight. It's a Para thing. Anyway that's it out of my system for another ten years or so. I suppose that's me off your list of possibles for good then?"

"Not for good, but certainly for a week or two."

Bernie smiled as she said it and walked back to her desk to get on with her work.

Frank was left on his own for the moment and wandered about vaguely trying to look busy. After a few minutes of that he decided to have a look at David's graph to see how much red there was left. It couldn't be much. He had been given a log-in of his own which allowed him access to the graph and websites he had needed for some of the testing and he signed in to have a look. After the usual wait the graph came up.

Frank stared at it looking for any areas of red in the rectangle but he couldn't see any at all. After a while he gave up. Just as he was about to sign off he noticed a message underneath the graph which read, "testing complete". That was strange. If it was complete surely he could head off. There had been mention earlier of keeping him about till they were 100% sure they had his full brain activity recorded but this suggested that they already did. He looked up and saw that Bobby had come into the suite and was talking to David.

Frank walked over and when they finished their chat he said: "The graph in the computer looks like it's complete. It even says so underneath. What exactly do you need me for this afternoon?"

David looked at Bobby who took the lead.

"Technically we have finished recording the full spectrum of your brain's activity, that is true, however we are keen to compare David's result's with the comparative study I have been working on in D Section. The best way is to retest some specific brain activity using the equipment there in order to ensure we are comparing like for like between the two studies."

Bobby paused and stared at Frank. Frank stared back. It all sounded fair enough to him.

"So I'll be heading down to D Section with you and there I'll be wired up to an identical set of scanners?"

"Yes," said Bobby. "We have prepared a programme of specific cross sections of what has been tested here and we will induce a small period of sleep while we run it. It should only take about half an hour or so. You'll need an hour to come to afterwards."

Frank paused again. "And then we're done and I can go home?"

"Yes," said Bobby again. "We are really pleased with the way you have helped us I have to say. I have taken the liberty of adding a little bonus to your fee as a way of saying thank you."

"Fair enough," said Frank, "when do we start?"

"No time like the present. The team may well be away or busy when you finish so best say your goodbyes now."

Frank nodded, distracted by the thought of the added bonus. Maybe a holiday with Charlotte was on the cards. Sounds like he could afford it.

He turned to the team who had been summoned by David and thanked them all as he shook their hands. He managed not to wince as Shona insisted on giving him a big hug of farewell but was glad when Bernie followed suit. David give him a big grin as he shook his hand at the end of the line-up

"It's been a pleasure. I am really excited by what we can work on now and a lot of that is down to you."

"It has been fun," said Frank, not necessarily meaning his time in the Penicuik suite, but thinking rather of the whole three weeks.

Chapter Eighteen

As the days passed and Blaine's excitement and enthusiasm grew, Delores seemed to be pushed further and further to the side. During the day she had nothing to do. She played no part in the scientific aspects of Blaine's preparation. In the evenings they would meet up in the apartment and talk but seemed to have less and less in common. Blaine was still guarded about the treatment and she resented being kept out of the loop. She also noticed how his mood had improved recently. Bobby had warned her that Blaine's painkillers were going to be increased and she might see some personality changes. Changes which would continue after the treatment too. But there was more to it than that. Blaine was starting to enjoy his involvement with Nebus Bioscience. He seemed to look forward to the days in the labs and less to their time together in the evening.

Eventually Delores felt sufficiently excluded to give Blaine an ultimatum.

"I know you have a lot on your mind honey but I need to be involved. I need to know what you are thinking. I appreciate this chance of survival is an opportunity for you; for us. But I feel left out of what's going on. I need to know you still feel the same way about me and our future together."

Blaine looked at her and was a little bit taken aback. He had been in an adrenalin fuelled world of science and selfishness and knew he had been neglecting her.

"Of course I still love you honey," he replied. "I don't want to leave you out of anything in my life but there are risks with this treatment as well as the possibilities and I would rather face them alone. We'll be together full time soon enough; I just have to focus on what lies ahead for now to make sure that happens. I know you feel left out but ultimately this stage is all about my body and there is nothing you need to do on the practical side of things. But I need to know you'll be there for me afterwards."

Delores nodded. She wasn't convinced.

"I thought I might go and visit my sister in Atlanta for the last week and then head back after your treatment is finished. Until then I don't know what good I can be to you."

If she had hoped Blaine might try to talk her out of it she was sadly disappointed.

"Okay honey. If that's what you want. You must be bored rigid here at the moment. Come back when I'm through it all and then we can be together."

Delores nodded agreement although inside she felt angry. She didn't even know if her sister was home. She stood up kissed him on the forehead and headed for the door.

Realising his lack of concern too late Blaine stood up too and moved to intercept her before she reached the door. As he did so though he felt himself go light headed and grabbed at the table, knocking his plate onto the floor with a crash.

Delores spun round to see him struggling for balance and rushed back to help him back into his seat.

"I'm sorry sweetheart," she said. "I keep forgetting how ill you are. I'm selfish; please forgive me."

Back on his seat Blaine quickly recovered. He held her hand and pulled her down beside him till he could kiss her face.

"I've been selfish too," he said. "Go and visit your sister. This stage is all routine but must be boring as hell for you. I'm in very capable hands here. When this is all done, that's when I'll need you most."

He kissed her face again and she helped him over to the bed to lie down. He felt well enough recovered that he didn't actually need to but he had regained her sympathy and was not going to blow it again. He closed his eyes once he was safely on the bed and lay still as Delores removed his shoes. She kissed him on the lips and quietly made her way out of the flat to the waiting transport.

Once she had left Blaine opened his eyes again, sat up slowly this time and headed for the sofa to watch some TV. He wasn't that tired yet.

The next day Delores booked a flight for that evening before going to see Blaine. They had lunch together and she confirmed she would be heading off to visit her sister in Atlanta as discussed (Fortunately her sister had been about). They made small talk till it was time for Blaine to go back to the Nebraska Suite. She noticed he looked much better than he had the night before and hoped he could keep his spirits up for the battle ahead. It seemed as though he would be able to cope better without her at this stage and although that disappointed her she felt she understood. She was a diversion, perhaps and he needed to focus on the goal.

They kissed tenderly but quickly as they parted and he whispered in her ear that he loved her. She mouthed the same back before turning towards the exit. Now she had something to do she felt better. Delores was fairly close to her sister but hadn't managed to visit her or her kids for over two years. She had never been a big fan of her brother in law but it sounded like he was away on business and they could have a proper catch up together. She headed out through the door without turning round and focused on the journey ahead. She was looking forward to a distraction and getting back to the states.

Blaine watched her go and breathed out. Yes he loved her but with everything that lay ahead and no option for the moment of explaining the details to her he had felt boxed in when they were together. It would be different once everything was over and done with. Or at least he hoped it would be. Either way he could concentrate on the recording and mapping sessions without any diversions now and unwind at the end of each day in his own company.

The following week passed quickly and Blaine watched till all the areas of the graph had turned green. Bobby was pleased at the progress they had made and confirmed that he and his team would spend the next day checking and double checking the data. If everything was in order the transfer would be carried out the day after that.

Blaine was still excited although his body had adjusted to the new painkiller regime and he was no longer euphoric. The pains in his back and neck were still there but were bearable. His main problem was the grinding fatigue of getting through each day. If the transfer worked out okay and he regained his former energy levels or better, then it would have been worth it just for that.

He spent the next day in the apartment largely alone. Bobby had popped in as had Dan very briefly. Nick the minder had checked every few hours to see if he wanted anything and had organised food for roughly each mealtime. Blaine wasn't hungry though and had only been able to toy with each plateful. He was far too on edge to eat or focus on anything but the next day's procedure.

What would it be like to inhabit a different body? How easily could he adjust? A thousand possible situations popped into his head and he tried each time to think them through logically. Eventually though he realised that there was no way on earth he could prepare himself accurately. Whatever it would feel like would happen and he would just have to deal with it.

Bobby had left a sleeping pill for him with the advice that he take it. Blaine knew it was good advice. With his brain rushing around with so many unanswerable questions it would be the only way of getting anything like a good night's sleep. He took the pill at around half past nine in the evening, having given up trying to follow a film on TV. Even with the soporific effects of the drug it took a while before he drifted off to sleep. But in the end he did and slept right through till the next morning.

He awoke before his alarm went off but only just. Today was the big day he thought to himself. He shaved and showered more carefully than usual. Strange as it seemed when he thought about it, he wanted his body as clean and tidy as it could be for its new owner. He had a light breakfast he headed over to Bobby's office as agreed. Bobby checked him over again and then explained that the procedure would not take place till late in the afternoon as the donor had to go through some minor checks. Deflated Blaine plodded back to his room where he kicked his heals impatiently for several hours. He tried and failed to get interested in daytime TV, or a book or any of the magazines in the apartment. He even struggled to focus on the latest financial figures from Nebus. He showered another twice before the appointed time eventually arrived and he could head back to Bobby's office.

Bobby was keen to coordinate everyone's movements and ensure that timings were strictly adhered to. He emphasised again that it was important that Blaine and the donor didn't meet prior to the transfer taking place and kept him in his office till a phone call confirmed that the donor was safely in room B of the suite.

Together the two men walked the short distance to the Nebraska Suite and entered. Blaine looked over at room B and wondered what was going through the mind of that poor son of a bitch. Deluded he must be and desperate too but Blaine felt sorry none the less.

Between rooms A and B were a group of Bobby's team members. They didn't look up or acknowledge the new arrivals. They seemed tense and entirely focussed on what each of them had to do. Computer screens were being checked, clipboards signed and passed around and short confirmatory conversations taking place throughout the room. Blaine noticed that his minder Nick was standing talking to another heavy set individual and that the two security personnel had positioned themselves exactly between the two rooms. It looked for all the world as if they were standing guard to keep the occupants of each room separate.

Bobby led Blaine into Room A and signalled that he should get up on the table. One of the men in white coats who were already in the room helped him up and then started connecting up the now familiar equipment. Once it was all in place and the team had run through a series of tests and checks, most of them left the room.

Bobby walked over to Blaine and smiled. It was a fairly thin unconvincing smile but he was obviously giving it his best shot at reassurance.

"Everything is ready here and next door," he said to Blaine, still trying to smile as he spoke. "I am very confident in this procedure and so should you be. In a few hours you will wake up in the donor's body with a long and healthy life ahead of you. Now please take this sedative, lie back and relax."

Blaine did as he was told and felt the feeling of handing over all responsibility return. He liked the feeling. It was similar to being a passenger on an aircraft. His safety, health and future were now in the hands of somebody else. There was nothing he could do. Nothing he should do. Just relax and let it all happen. The sedative kicked in and he drifted off into a deep sleep. He dreamt happy dreams and then all of a sudden was aware that he was not dreaming at all. A strange feeling of limbo somehow. Then he was aware of nothing till he started to come round some time later.

Chapter Nineteen

Bobby led the way out of the suite and round the corridors to D Section. He didn't say anything as they went and seemed a little bit nervous but Frank didn't care. One afternoon's kip and he was offsky home.

They arrived at the secure reception area and Dr Bobby motioned him through the doors as the security guys opened it for them. No questions were asked regarding Frank's right of access. Clearly Bobby ruled the roost here.

As they went through the door into D Section Frank was a bit disappointed. He wasn't sure what he had expected but D section was pretty much a copy of the rest of the building. He followed Bobby Bartleman along a corridor identical to the ones he had become used to until they arrived at a "The Nebraska Suite", which was remarkably similar to the Penicuik suite. Inside there was a similar arrangement of desks and computers with a number of people working at them, none of whom looked up as he and Bobby entered. At the far end of the suite were two rooms, just like the Penicuik suite, but as he approached he noticed that instead of one being a gym and the other one the bedroom-like area which had been used to record his sleeping brain's activity, here both rooms were set up with tables and the familiar recording equipment. Someone had imaginatively named them Room A and Room B.

Bobby led the way to room B. Inside it, a number of people were waiting around the equipment beside the table and they at least looked up and nodded to Frank. He nodded back but didn't smile. It looked like that was forbidden in D section.

"If you like to jump up on the table as usual we will get you all connected up. You know the drills by now. We will need you to doze off so if you could just swallow this mild sedative that should do it."

One of the men in white lab coats handed him a small pill and a glass of water. Frank popped the pill in his mouth and washed it down with a sip of water then returned the glass.

"Thanks," said the man in a broad American accent.

Frank hopped onto the table and the team started to connect him to the apparatus. He noticed as they worked and spoke to him and to each other that they were all Americans. It made no difference to him he thought. If that's where the money came from he didn't mind working for the Yankee dollar. As they were finishing the connections and checking the screens at the side of the room, Frank felt the sedative start to take effect. First of all he found his concentration on what was happening around him fading a bit, then his head slipped to one side a few times then he was asleep. He dreamed of chess and exercising in a gym, of going through basic training again, of women, of fights and then of nothing at all. Somehow though he was aware that he was dreaming of nothing. It was a strange sensation but he could do nothing about it. He was conscious but aware of his brain being unconscious at the same time. He could hear nothing, feel nothing and sense nothing.

Then he must have gone into a deeper sleep because the sensation ended and he was conscious of nothing. Then he dreamed some more. This time his dreams were about shouting at his group on the seafront at Ayr, as they coughed and wheezed through a workout on a cold, winter's morning before they headed for work. He noticed Charlotte was in the group. "Strange," he thought, but kept on shouting and berating them all.

Then Frank began to wake up. He was groggy at first and felt dreadful. It wasn't just that his mouth was dry and his head was sore. No, there was something else not well about him. He had a pain in his stomach and his neck. It felt like it had been there for a while but he knew that couldn't be the case. He was more than just drowsy from the sleeping pill. He felt deep down tired like he had been exercising for days or fighting a cold or the flu and losing. He raised his head slightly from the pillow with difficulty and looked round expecting to see Dr Bobby but he wasn't there. In fact none of the team were there in the room with him. The only person there was a security guard he had never seen before.

"Take it easy," the guard said in a definite, American, southern drawl. "Just take your time and get your breath back."

Frank noticed the instruction was said without any friendliness or concern. He looked round the room as far as he could see it from the table and noticed the two way mirror was on the opposite side now. At first he thought the table must have been turned around but the main entrance door was still in the same place. The only explanation he could come up with was that he was now in Room A. For some reason Bobby and his team must have put him into the neighbouring room to recuperate. Again he tried to raise his head but it hurt too much and his whole body was too drained to achieve even this simple task. "Christ," he thought to himself, "they had really got their money's worth out of him this time."

He waited till he felt slightly more awake even if he didn't feel in any better health and tried to raise his head again. This time he managed to raise it off the table and look down his body to the other end of the room. Something immediately struck him as he did so. He was no longer wearing the blue sweater and grey trousers he had been wearing when he arrived that day. Wait a minute he thought. Someone's changed my clothes while I slept. He looked down again and saw that he was wearing a smart tweed jacket with a hound's-tooth checked shirt underneath. On his lower half he had a pair of brown cords. I hate brown cords, he thought to himself. Then he realised something else. In order to see the trousers he had to lift his head above the level of a definite beer gut. "What the fuck?"

How long had he been asleep, he wondered. What had they done to him? He had to stand up and find out what was going on. He tried but was still too weak.

"Just relax buddy, the doc will be alone to explain what happens next," the guard said. "Till then just relax."

"I'll relax you in a minute," thought Frank but knew he would have to feel a whole lot better to floor this guy but looked forward to the prospect. For now he had enough to worry about. He had gone to sleep feeling as fit as a fiddle wearing a blue sweater and grey trousers, close to his natural fighting weight. He had now woken up wearing an admittedly expensive looking jacket and cords ensemble and feeling like shit. He also appeared to have put on enough weight to need the cords to be five sizes larger than the slacks he had put on that morning. Nothing made sense. He had to find Bobby and ask what the hell was going on. He tried to sit up with enough determination this time to move most of his torso before giving up.

"Look McCoard, you ain't going anywhere till the doc says so. I know you like causing trouble and if you want it that's fine by me. Got to say you let yourself go since you were in the forces. Wouldn't take much to put you down now."

Frank tried to speak but his throat was too dry. Who the fuck was McCoard?

With a superhuman effort to clear his throat he managed to rasp out: "Who the fuck is McCoard. My name's Chisholm, Frank Chisholm."

"Look buddy, all I know is that your badge says Blaine McCoard and the picture is a dead ringer, so you're McCoard. Either way you ain't moving till the doc gets back and he says I've to ensure that, whatever it takes. Get my drift?"

Frank hadn't a clue what this clown was talking about but if he wanted a scrap Frank would oblige just as soon as he could move.

"The name's Chisholm you arsehole," he managed to say.

He felt the guard grab the back of his head roughly and with his other hand hold the security badge in front of his face.

"You're McCoard," he said. "Says so here buddy, just under that fat face of yours."

He let Frank's head fall without supporting it and it hit the table painfully.

Frank was confused. The badge had a picture of a completely different guy on it. The guard was either blind or stupid. The picture showed a man who slightly resembled him in terms of age perhaps, but was overweight and a bit jowly. At least one other chin was showing under the main one.

"That looks nothing like me you stupid bastard. I want to see Dr Robert Bartleman and I want to see him now."

There was a strange tone to Frank's voice that was not simply explained by the dryness in his mouth. Just speaking felt strange and if he didn't know any better he would have said there was a hint of an accent there too. He had been here too long he thought to himself.

Before he had time to think about it any further he felt his head being grasped again and saw the guard shove the badge in front of his face again.

"Look wise guy, your badge looks like this and," he let the badge go and held up a small shaving mirror in front of Frank's face, "you look like this too. I wouldn't like to look like you either but them's the breaks. If you don't settle down and stop calling me names I might forget to be so nice to you."

Again the guard dropped Frank's head with a bump. This time he didn't notice. He was stunned. In the mirror he had expected to see that loveable rogue Frank "the tank" Chisholm's face but instead had seen the same face as was on the badge. A chubby stranger wearing a tweed jacket and hound's-tooth check shirt. For a minute sheer panic set in. Frank still couldn't move very much but he knew something was badly wrong. How could he have turned into someone else? It was impossible. He tried to comfort himself with the thought that he was still dreaming but he knew he wasn't.

He lay there for some time trying to figure out what had happened but he could not. He felt less drowsy now but the whole situation made him sick with fear. There was still an underlying sense of being ill somehow which wasn't going but he knew he was getting the ability to move back in his body and legs. He had to think this through and he had to find Dr Bobby fucking Bartleman. If he could get enough strength back in his legs he could maybe...

Before he was able to come up with a plan he heard the door opening behind him and one of the men in white lab coats came back in.

"How are you feeling?" he asked, again without any trace of concern in his voice.

"Actually I'm not feeling myself at the moment," Frank replied hoping he could get some information from this guy with a little bit of charm and humour.

"That's hardly surprising all things considered." the American replied. He looked over at the guard and said,

"You can have a break now. Mr McCoard will be harmless for a while yet."

The guard looked at Frank, smiled then left the room.

"Now I want to tell you a little story," began the man in the lab coat. "Once upon a time there was a very important man who was really quite ill. He had some powerful friends who needed him to live a long and prosperous life. There was another man who was a thick ex-airborne soldier who happened to match the important man in many ways. The man's friends found a way of swapping them over so that the important man got a healthy body and lived happily ever after and the poor old soldier didn't. Any of this ring a bell?"

Frank struggled to believe what he was being told but Dan Bartleman continued. "The poor soldier got a body dying of cancer and was flown back to the States where he very soon died, tragically, before he could even see his wife and kids again. This made them very sad indeed but he had been well insured so they were able to live happily ever after too. The important man was also able to go to the States and start a new life with a beautiful new wife and continue to make lots and lots of money for his friends. In time his friends found people who were a perfect match for them and so they were able to live considerably longer and happier than they could previously have imagined."

Frank didn't like what he was hearing. He still hoped it was a dream but it was seeming more and more like a nightmare all the time.

"You're telling me you swapped my body with someone else. Someone dying of cancer," he managed to gasp out.

"Yes, although now that we have been successful he is no longer dying of cancer. You are! Sorry Frank, you just happened to be the perfect match for a very important person within my corporation. I can't afford to lose them and their ability to make money. So you lucked out."

That explained the illness Frank had felt when he woke up again. They hadn't wheeled him to another room. They'd stolen his personality and shoved it into the dying body of a fat American businessman. The fat businessman was presumably relaxing in Frank's body so he could go on making money for these people. Frank had been afraid before but now he was spitting mad and made a grab for Dan's arm. Although he caught it he was way too weak to do anything and Dan, aged as he was, batted the hand away without difficulty.

"Now, now Frank," he said. "You are not the man you once were. Even when you get the hang of your new body it won't be a match for Claude, who will be making sure you get safely back to the states whether you like it or not. I warn you, from his background, he might rather enjoy you trying to put up a fight."

Frank sank back onto the table, crushed for the moment by his predicament. He couldn't even grab and hold onto this old man never mind sort out the useful looking guard he now had in tow. Amazing as the old man's story had been it seemed to be the only way of explaining things. He felt ill, was now overweight and looked different to the man he had shaved that morning. He was even wearing a stranger's clothes. Cords for Christ sake. None of this was good.

Claude returned and sat down again, picking up a magazine as he did so.

"Make sure Mr McCoard remains here till his transport arrives. Dr Bartleman will be back then. I gather there was a delay with the ambulance so you may have a bit of a wait." After that the old man in the lab coat left the room

Frank assumed Claude had nodded. He certainly didn't say anything. If he thought he was guarding someone called McCoard then maybe Claude wasn't up to speed on exactly what had happened. Maybe Frank could persuade him to help. He looked out of the corner of his eye at his jailer and decided that was unlikely. If Claude had a decent streak in him it was well hidden even assuming Frank could convince him of the truth. No, it looked like Claude was going to be loyal to his bosses whatever. Frank would need a different plan to get out of this fix and quickly.

Chapter Twenty

Blane slowly opened his eyes and looked up. Bobby Bartleman was standing on one side of him and his uncle Dan on the other. There was one other person in the room. Nick the security guard.

"Just relax and take things easy," Robby said. "How do you feel?"

"Surprisingly good. And pain free," said Blaine whispered, still drowsy from the sedative.

"You now have to make some adjustments mentally and get used to your new... surroundings."

Blaine tipped his head slightly and looked down at his body, or what he could see of it, which wasn't much. He expected to see the round shape of his stomach but could not. He tried to sit up but was still too sedated to move much. He managed to move his hands slightly and felt his waist and the belt of his trousers. There was an unfamiliar feeling to the process. He knew he was still groggy from the drugs but there was more. The shape of his waist was quite different and the belt had a pattern to it proving it was not the one he had fastened that morning. Slowly he moved his hands over his stomach and chest and had a moment of panic. Bobby took his hand and held it for reassurance.

"How does it feel son?" asked Dan. "How do you feel?"

"Still groggy I guess," replied Blaine. "But there is no pain and I feel... healthy somehow."

"Good, good," said Dan. "Everything went smoothly son. The transfer was a huge success."

"Both ways?" asked Blaine.

"Sure of course. The donor switched too. He's fine. Just waking up slowly like you."

"Can I meet him?" asked Blaine.

"That wouldn't be wise at the moment," Bobby chipped in. "You both have a lot to come to terms with. Maybe in a week or two. Maybe not. For now just take your time and get used to your new host."

Bobby reached for a syringe which lay on a nearby table and, after ejecting a small spray to test it, he administered the contents into Blaine's arm.

"This will speed up the recovery from the sedative. Now we know you're okay."

Dan nodded at Nick the security guard who casually left the room.

Whatever had been in the syringe had a rapid effect on Blaine. After a further five minutes he was able to raise his head and look down at the new body he was inhabiting. Although the sensations he felt were utterly strange in some ways, in others it was very much what he had expected. The pains from his cancer were gone. He felt a wellbeing throughout his body that he had not known since his early days at university, playing soccer. He moved his hands and looked at them. They were no longer flabby and pasty in colour. The arms attached to them were toned and he could already feel the raw power they possessed. He moved his feet and legs slightly and although he couldn't see them yet, he could feel the same strength there too. Whatever they had had to pay this poor sap to give up his healthy body was money well spent for Blaine and nowhere enough for the donor.

After ten minutes or so he was able to sit up with Bobby's help. At first he was a little light-headed but that soon passed. He was able to move his arms and legs freely now and liked the feeling of power and health.

Another five minutes or so and he managed to stand with Bobby on one side and Dan on the other. They walked him round the room a couple of times as if trying to sober up a drunk. After two and a half laps of the room Blaine was able to walk slowly on his own. As he walked he noticed the room he was in now was a mirror image of the one he had entered. This must be Room B he thought.

He made his way to the bathroom, knowing from his previous visits that there was a mirror there. Bobby followed him at this point, concerned about Blaine's reaction to the first sight of his new face. Blaine slowly moved to a position in front of the mirror and stared open mouthed. Gone were the fat jowls and baggy eyes he was used to. Instead there was a face clearly of similar age to him. But this one had no spare flesh at all. The broken nose might take a bit of getting used to, he thought, but he could live with the rest. The big question was, could Delores.

He turned to Bobby and Dan and smiled, giving them a thumbs up. Bobby breathed an audible sigh of relief and turned to Dan with a smile. Dan was beaming from ear to ear.

"He's an ugly son of a bitch," laughed Blaine, "but he'll do."

"We'll have you back at the reigns of Nebus in no time," said Dan still smiling at how well his plans were going.

The three men made their way to Bobby's office with much back patting and joviality stemming from a collective sense of relief. At the office Bobby gave Blaine a quick medical check, which confirmed what he already knew to the n'th degree: Frank's body was as fit as a fiddle.

They discussed the next stage in detail. The three of them would head off to Glasgow the next day and spend the night there. Delores would fly in and join them there. Bobby would explain what had taken place to her and gauge her reaction. Assuming she was still on board she would join Blaine and head off for two weeks R & R at a health resort Nebus owned in the Highlands. All being well Blaine could then start to take up the reigns again at Nebus. Initially by email and fax with Delores doing any actual talking, till his accent was under control again.

Blaine was nervous about meeting up with Delores again but overall he was too pleased at the way he felt to care. He was pain free, strong and fit like never before, or at least not for a long time. And now he was not going to die young. He felt completely euphoric and knew it had nothing to do with any drugs or medication this time. His life would go on now, one way or another. He had been reprieved from a death sentence and everything and everyone else was secondary to that fact.

After the details were agreed Dan stood up as if about to make a speech.

"I was hoping things would turn out this way and have prepared a little surprise. Please follow me to the restaurant if you will." And with that he led the way through the door of Bobby's office and down the corridor towards the main entrance to Section D.

He swept the other two men along with him through the security door and past the night guard on duty there.

The guard was the large individual called Greg who had taken an instant dislike to Frank. When he saw what he took to be Frank waltz through the door with two of the big bosses and smile a hello at him he assumed he was taking the piss. His face fixed into a forced grin and he stared with undisguised malice at big Frank. "Just one little excuse," he thought to himself, "and I'll sort you right out."

Blaine for his part had smiled at the guard in all innocence. He was surprised and disappointed not to get the usual polite smile back and sensed an element of hostility directed towards him. Not to worry, he thought. Can't be easy staying there all night with nothing to do.

Dan led the way to the canteen where an area had been screened off near the kitchen. As they entered the newly formed dining room Blaine noticed that a table had been set for three with a proper cloth, cutlery, china and crystal glasses. A rather gaudy candelabra decorated the middle of it but the overall effect was impressive.

"I thought the three of us should celebrate." Dan said. "After all I regard this as representing a new era for Nebus. Of course the main point is that our most successful CEO to date is healthy again and will be with us for many years to come."

He walked over to a side table and picked up a bottle of Champagne. He opened it with practiced skill and poured three generous glasses. Handing one to each of his companions, he took the third himself.

"I propose a toast. To Bobby and his team who have ensured your survival Blaine, and shown the way forward for Nebus management into the future."

They all raised their glasses and drank some champagne. Dan indicated for the other two to sit and rang a small bell which sat beside his place. A waiter appeared with plates containing starters of grilled scallops in a ginger jus, set on the plates like a sculpture amidst an exotic salad. The three men, suddenly aware that they were very hungry and hadn't eaten for some time, tucked in.

Blaine wasn't entirely sure what Dan had meant with his toast but he knew he felt good and he knew he was hungry.

The three of them enjoyed a lavish meal which Dan had obviously taken great pains to organise and each course was accompanied by the perfect and most expensive of wines. As the food went down and the wine took effect they talked and joked louder and louder. Time went by without them noticing its passing until eventually Blaine had to call a halt. Healthy and fit as he was he suddenly felt the need to lie down. He was also surprised at how much he was enjoying drinking the wines and realised he had consumed far more than he normally would.

Dan suggested he go back to the apartment and lie down. There had been a delay with the transport for the donor and he wanted to discuss it with Bobby. They all stood up hugged and slapped each other's backs again. Then Blaine headed, slightly unsteadily, towards the stairs and D Section. He gathered his focus and made it slowly down to the bottom. A strange regret entered his head about not taking a bottle of wine with him to his room but he dismissed it and headed towards his bed.

As he turned the corner towards the security gate he saw the guard look up and eye him suspiciously. It was at that moment that it dawned on him that he didn't have his own security badge. The one round his neck said Frank Chisholm visitor and Sections A-C only written on it. Blaine was sure that wouldn't be a problem with the big man at reception.

The big man at reception had very different ideas. Here came that Chisholm guy without his friends and it looked like he was going to try and get into D Section without permission. Christmas had come early.

"You are not allowed into this area without authority," he growled at what he assumed was Frank.

Blaine was annoyed at the man's tone. "Just let me through if you know what's good for you," he replied.

"Like that is it," thought the guard.

"You are not getting past me without authority to enter this area and you don't have it mate."

"Just get out of my way," said Blaine angry and emboldened by the amount of wine he had had.

The guard stood up and blocked the way through as Blaine arrived at the desk. Blaine pushed at the guard roughly but didn't manage to get him out of the way.

"You asked for it," said the guard and took a swing at Frank's head.

Before Blaine had time to think about it he had ducked to one side, missing the blow and countered with a vicious left jab which took the guard completely by surprise and knocked him out cold.

Blaine paused and looked at the prone figure at his feet in surprise. Then he stared at his fist and smiled. "I really enjoyed that," he thought to himself.

He pushed the button on the desk to open the security door and headed off to the apartment for a well deserved rest. Pity there wasn't any more drink there he found himself thinking. But the bed looked too welcoming and he lay down on it and slept almost immediately.

Chapter Twenty One

Frank started moving his limbs slightly; testing them and trying to gauge how effective they were as the sedative slowly wore off. It seemed like they were all working again but he found it impossible to figure out how strong his new body was and how effective it would be in a fight with Claude. Not very, was his over-riding conclusion but that just meant it couldn't be a fair fight.

Once he was sure that his new body would at least move when he wanted it to, he decided that if he was to have a chance of avoiding the fatal trip to the States he better act now or never. He cleared his throat to make sure he could speak.

"I need to go for a pee," he said. "You'll need to help me stand up."

Claude looked up and reluctantly put his magazine down, walked over and helped Frank sit up. Frank noticed the magazine was an issue of Muscle and Fitness which didn't give him any greater confidence in his plan succeeding. He moved to the edge of the table he had been lying on and stretched one leg so that it touched the floor. He shuffled forward and put the other foot down as well. Frank felt himself being roughly pulled upright and onto his feet. He swayed a bit and for a split second thought he was going to fall over but managed to get his balance and remain standing. Slowly he put one foot forward and then the other making slow progress towards the bathroom. All the time he moved he was trying to assess how useful this new body could be. It was not fit to say the least, but its very weight might give him some kind of advantage. He was moving slowly and cautiously but guessed he could move a bit faster if he needed to. The limbs all worked as they should and he was now quite confident of his balance.

Claude watched his captive's progress all the way. Whatever he had been through medically and whatever he had been in the past, this McCoard guy didn't look like he could cause any trouble. He had done a few jobs for Nebus over the years when they needed extra security for staff at home or abroad or wanted someone scared off, but this looked like being the easiest money yet. Get this walking corpse over to the States and hand him over to some other freelance security guys there. Piece of cake. If it all went to plan he could be having a beer in his favourite sports bar the following night cheering on the Red Sox.

Frank closed the door of the bathroom behind him and nearly fainted at the face looking back at him in the mirror. Instead of Frank "the tank" Chisholm's cheeky grin there was a pallid and chubby face staring back. There were certain similarities it was true but this was a cruel caricature of his former self.

He dragged his eyes away from the mirror and looked around the bathroom. There wasn't much to see. A toilet, a sink and a shower with some towels over a towel rail which was firmly attached to the wall. Then he noticed that the toilet roll holder on the wall was broken and somebody had kindly brought in a floor standing version to replace it. Presumably this was a temporary arrangement till someone with clearance to work in D Section could get round to fixing it. Frank examined it closely. It was a stainless steel affair with a D shaped loop at the top for the toilet roll itself. There was a long, narrow barrel-like piece under that which connected to a circular base plate on the floor. Frank tried it for weight and liked it. The British army had never trained him to use a toilet roll holder as a weapon of choice but the base plate was fairly heavy and sharp at the edge. He lifted it over his head and waived it around a couple of times to make sure it would hold together. It seemed well-constructed as these things go and Frank decided this was his best chance of escape.

There was no lock on the door allowing any guard to check on who was inside and what they were doing Frank had noticed. He hit his new weapon off the floor and shouted to Claude outside, "Help, I've fallen over! I need help!"

Outside Claude was starting to get pissed off with this McCoard guy. He put his magazine down again and walked to the toilet. If that lame son of a bitch had fallen over and pissed himself he was getting left where he'd dropped till it was time to head for the airport. If he hadn't, he was going to get dragged back to the bed and hurt on the way. He straightened his jacket and reached for the door handle.

Inside the bathroom Frank waited with the toilet roll holder above his head. He knew that he would get one go at this and that if he didn't put Claude down first time he would get a severe beating and any chance of escape would have gone.

He watched the handle of the door turn and as an angry Claude appeared through the open door Frank brought the improvised club down on the top of his head as hard as he could. It connected with the guards head with a loud thump and Frank knew the sharp edge of the base had dug in deep. For a second Claude just stood there with his angry face staring at his attacker.

"Shit", thought Frank, "He's not going down."

He frantically raised the weapon and was surprised that he was able to and to land another blow without Claude moving a muscle. He must have been stunned from the first blow. The second time the base of the toilet roll holder connected with Claude's head it had the desired effect. His legs gave way first and then he slumped to the floor unconscious.

If anyone had asked him later Frank would have admitted that the next two blows were gratuitous but he was in no mood to take chances and didn't want to risk his guard coming round any time soon and raising the alarm.

He pulled the body into the bathroom hoping the blood outside would not be noticed. The amount of blood inside could not be missed but there wasn't time to do anything about that. Frank closed the door of the bathroom as he left it and took stock. He was uninjured but still fairly weak. He could move reasonably well and behave as if he was fine should he have to. A quick search of Claude had revealed no weapons, which was a disappointment but he decided he probably had to get out of here using brains rather than brawn.

He moved quickly over to the door and tried the handle. The door was electronically locked. He swiped the badge which was round his neck and could have shouted with joy as he heard the unmistakable click as the lock was released. Opening the door he looked out. The suite was empty. He risked a quick look through the door of Room B, but it was deserted too.

"Body snatching bastards," he whispered under his breath and headed to the exit of the Nebraska suite. He opened the door and looked outside. Again there was nobody about. He could see the main entrance to D Section and knew there would be guards outside. It was a huge risk but he guessed the British guards at reception weren't in on what had happened inside, in which case they should be cool with an American businessman with rights of access leaving the area. Hopefully they were focused on people trying to get in rather than those exiting through the door.

Frank took a deep breath, straightened has jacket and shirt and headed to the door. He pressed the open button and walked through as nonchalantly as possible. There was one guard sitting in the usual position beside the desk. Frank tensed himself ready for any awkwardness but there was none. Instead the guard gave him a respectful smile and said, "Goodnight Mr McCoard."

Frank was not confident enough of his voice and accent yet so he simply smiled back and gave a mock salute. The guard smiled, returned a similar mock salute and went back to reading his newspaper.

Frank waited till he was round the corner before breathing out a huge sigh of relief. That was easy enough he thought. He continued towards the main reception where he knew at this time of night another guard would be on duty. As he passed, the guard again looked up and smiled. Frank smiled and nodded back. At last these bastards were showing him a bit of respect.

He walked to the front door and out of the building with no clear plan of what to do next. He vaguely knew he needed help which meant Paddy but how the hell could he explain the fact that he had been transferred against his will into a fat American's body. Paddy was ready for most things but this would be a step too far. He also knew he needed to get away from the Nebus plant quickly and buy time to think things through including some way of getting Paddy onboard. He checked his pockets for money to see if he could afford a taxi. He found a wallet with £500 in new twenty pound notes and a similar sum in dollars. That should get him back to Ayr. The hotel was a non-starter for now. Whatever the plan had been, Bobby and his American friends would have arranged something to sort his checking out without raising suspicions. Chances are the staff at the hotel would be so pleased to be rid of him they would ask no questions whatsoever.

As he walked away from the building towards the main road he suddenly noticed a dark people carrier with the courtesy light on. Surely it couldn't be his old pal Jim. But it was. Frank was just about to run over to the vehicle and jump in when he remembered that he now looked completely different to their last meeting. That was a pity he thought to himself with major understatement. Still, he was sure Jim would not be in on the dodgy dealings of D Section and might be persuaded to give Mr Blaine McCoard a lift somewhere, even if not all the way to Ayr itself.

Frank tapped the window and Jim looked up from his book. He lowered the window and said, "Can I help you?"

Looks like he doesn't know who I am thought Frank.

"I'm Blaine McCoard and I need to get to Ayr in a hurry. Are you free to take me?" Frank asked.

"I'm booked for a trip to the Crowne Plaza Hotel, Glasgow. It has been delayed for three hours but it's too tight for Ayr in between. I can check in with Dr Bartleman if you like."

"No need, I've just left him in D Section and he might be all night now." Frank bluffed. "They suggested I take their lift which must mean you and head over to the Nebus plant in Old Cumnock. There's a big problem there I need to sort."

Jim looked at him, shrugged his shoulders and told his unexpected passenger to jump in. It made no difference to him. He was scheduled to be available all night for D Section personnel and one was as good as another. A trip all the way to Ayr and back would break the monotony of the shift.

He sneaked a quick look at the American as he made a meal of climbing into the passenger seat; "jump in" seemed ambitious in retrospect. Once his passenger had finally got in and put his seatbelt on, Jim pulled smoothly away from the car park and headed out of the industrial estate. He noticed the American kept looking back nervously as if expecting someone to follow them but nobody did. Either way his badge said access all areas which told Jim he was important, so no point asking any questions.

Frank relaxed a little with every mile travelled. He had felt clumsy and awkward getting into the people carrier but overall he had got the hang of his new body. He had even got the drop on Claude he thought and giggled out loud. He looked at Jim and was about to take up where their previous conversation had ended but stopped himself just in time. After a while though, he started to ask Jim about his job and family. Jim covered ground Frank already knew but it was good just to talk to somebody. The conversation drifted into sport and "soccer" in particular. Jim was very impressed by this American's knowledge of Scottish football, including its rivalries and slang. He should meet big Frank, Jim thought to himself, they'd get on like a house on fire.

The journey took almost two hours but passed quicker than either had expected as they discussed their favourite moments in Scottish football. As they arrived at the Ayr by-pass Frank had a thought.

"Can you take me to the station please? I'm meeting someone there who'll drive me to the plant."

"No problem at all if you're sure they will be waiting?" Jim confirmed.

He turned and headed along the by-pass but half way along it, took the long road down into Ayr itself and pulled up at the railway station.

"This is perfect," said Frank in the strange mid-Atlantic accent he was having to get used to. He turned and shook Jim's hand. "Been a pleasure."

He then quickly hurried through the doors and into the station as if late for an appointment. Jim waited a few minutes just to be sure his passenger wasn't going to reappear and then headed off on the journey back towards Edinburgh.

Chapter Twenty Two

Blaine was woken what seemed like minutes later but was actually early next morning by a worried looking Bobby Bartleman.

"We have a bit of a problem," Bobby said. "The donor has disappeared."

Blaine's head was fuzzy with sleep and a hangover so it took a few seconds to remember everything that had happened.

"What do you mean disappeared?"

"He has left the building during the night after assaulting two of the guards, one British and one of our American staff. Apparently he persuaded our driver to take him to Ayr station and we have no trace of him since."

"How serious is that?" asked Blaine, "And how are the guards?"

"The British one is fine, just a sore jaw and damaged pride but Claude was seriously assaulted with a toilet roll holder."

There was a pause as Blaine stifled a laugh.

"It was a very heavy metal toilet roll holder and split his skull," clarified Bobby. "We've managed to deal with it here with all the medical staff we had on site. I've sent the Scottish guard home as he was a bit hazy about what actually happened. We need to move carefully till we find the donor again in case he is struggling to adjust. After all it has been quite a leap for everyone and we had hoped to monitor him for some time to come before helping him to readjust and settle down. Dan suggests we move to the hotel in Glasgow now and stay there till he's found. We'll take our security boys too as a precaution. Best get your stuff together so we can leave straight away."

Blaine did as he was told and packed some basics for the hotel. He realised quickly that none of the clothes he had left in the apartment fitted him properly anymore. The tops were tight on his new shoulders and hung loose over the toned muscles of his stomach. The trousers were ridiculously loose around his waist with the belts unable to close tightly enough to be of any use. Reluctantly he concluded that he would have to make do with Frank's taste in clothes for the journey but he resolved to send out from the hotel to get a replacement tweed jacket and some cords at the first opportunity.

When he was ready he made his way to Bobby's office as arranged and, along with Bobby, Dan and Nick the minder they made their way through a back entrance to a Range Rover with very dark windows which was waiting for them there. Nick got in and drove and Blaine noticed the large man in the passenger seat had his head covered in bandages and seemed to be heavily sedated.

"That must be Claude," he thought. "I wouldn't like to be in the donors shoes if he catches up with him." He shivered a bit when he realised that the donor only had Blaine's old physique at his disposal now. "Run fat boy run." he thought, and chuckled to himself.

They travelled largely in silence from the Nebus Biosciences plant to Glasgow. The Sat-Nav spoke more than any of the passengers. They turned off the M8 just before the Kingston Bridge and headed underneath it towards the newly developed riverside district. The Range Rover pulled up smoothly at The Crowne Plaza and they all got out except Nick who headed off to park the vehicle.

Bobby sorted out the rooms with reception who were expecting them although the Polish receptionist kept looking at Claude's bandaged head. Some of the bandages had traces of blood showing through. When Bobby emphasised that he was Dr Bartleman she relaxed visibly.

The group took the lift to the three rooms which had been booked together on the second top floor. Claude checked the first bedroom and ushered them in. He checked the other two and returned giving Dan a thumbs up sign. Blaine wasn't sure what Claude had expected to find but it looked like he had worked with Dan on a regular basis and was going through his usual routine. Probably as much as anything to prove the attack on his head had not had any lasting effect.

Claude took a chair from the room and positioned himself outside in the corridor.

"Is all this necessary?" Blaine asked.

"Not really," replied Dan, "but I think Claude is going overboard to regain our respect. Coming second best to a toilet roll holder wielded by an overweight businessman will take some time to come to terms with."

Dan laughed in a rather unkind way which suggested he had little sympathy with the poor man.

"I suggest we all settle into our rooms. I have some people looking for our donor in some of his old haunts and we can bring him in for further observation once they find him. In the meantime enjoy the views of Glasgow and whatever shitty little river that is out there until we can get back to civilisation. If you want some proper clothes Blaine, here's the number of a good concierge service in town my PA found for me. I suggest we reconvene here at six tonight and then go for dinner."

Bobby looked exhausted from what had obviously been a sleepless night and Blaine's hangover had not fully gone away so they headed off to their respective rooms to recover in their separate ways.

When Blaine had showered and had a nap he found himself again wanting a drink, which was strange. Not just a hair of the dog type desire. He wanted to get down to the bar and start another session. This was most unusual. He normally went days without having anything to drink and when he did he drank sparingly. Maybe it was just a temporary side effect of the transfer. But he found himself thinking again about flooring the night guard at Nebus Bioscience and decided he better watch out for any signs of new and dangerous habits. In the meantime though, a little something from the mini-bar would do no harm.

Shortly before 6.30 the three men met up again in Dan's room. Blaine had received a delivery of new clothes and had dressed in a pair of cords and a Tweed jacket which looked surprisingly like the one he had left behind in Room A on his old self. He felt better for wearing it but also for a rest and a shower. It had taken a bit of getting used to cleaning a new body but it emphasised to him his new found health and strength. Hopefully Delores would be suitably impressed too.

Dan was working away at the desk in is room when the other two arrived and didn't look up till he had dealt with a number of emails and finished a long and detailed phone call to his PA in the States. Eventually he looked up.

"We know the donor has been back to his house in Ayr and recovered his passport. Our people must have just missed him. It's a pity because we had hoped to use the passport to get you out of the country Blaine. Fortunately some of our official connections are organising a replacement one so that Frank Chisholm can officially travel to the States where he will disappear off the radar. At that point we can re-introduce you as Blaine McCoard. Fitter, slimmer and healthier perhaps but Blaine none the less. Ready to take up the overall reigns at Nebus holdings, on promotion."

Blaine liked the sound of that. So that had been Dan's plan if all went well. Move him to the parent company and run it. That would make the transition from married family man to carefree partner of the most beautiful employee in Nebus much easier. Things were coming together nicely, he thought. Maybe a drink was in order.

Chapter Twenty Three

Inside the station Frank peered round a corner where he could just see the reflection of the vehicle and waited till it drove away. When it did he waited another five minutes then hurried as best he could to his flat near the sea front. He quickly recovered the spare key from under the broken flower pot outside and let himself in. He moved cautiously at first just in case anyone on the Nebus payroll was waiting in the flat, but it was empty. Once he was sure of it he moved quicker, collecting some clothes, a hold-all and some washing and shaving kit. Finally he made his way to his bedroom and prised up one of the corner floorboards. Underneath was a bundle of ten pound notes totaling about £3,000 which he had kept from his boot camp sessions on the seafront. No need to tell the taxman about that. He reached further in to the gap where the floorboard had been until his hand felt the solid form of a pistol. It was a browning 9 mm pistol, standard issue in the British army, when he had been in, for anyone who didn't carry a rifle. He had found it during his second trip to the gulf and couldn't quite bring himself to hand it in. Had it been discovered in his kit at any time he would have been jailed forever but by a combination of cunning and good luck he had managed to bring it home as a trophy. Now for the first time he thought he might actually need it. He popped it into the bag with everything else and looked round. He had no idea what lay ahead but coming back to this flat and enjoying Coronation Street again on his sofa seemed an unlikely outcome.

He headed out of the flat as quickly and as quietly as he could and replaced the key under the plant pot out of sheer habit. His mind was racing now even if his new body couldn't quite keep up. He had to find Dr Bobby Bartleman and his team, track down his own body and make them reverse the whole routine. Sounded easy enough but getting everyone together again beside all the kit to make it happen seemed a virtual impossibility. But Frank had decided that if that proved impossible he was going to sort out all the bastards responsible. Bobby, the old boy from Room A who was probably his uncle and, one way or another, this bodysnatching McCoard guy.

He walked away from his flat and round a couple of corners to make sure he had not been followed. All of a sudden he was exhausted and knew he needed to rest. He flagged down a taxi and asked to be taken to the Premier Inn near the airport. The driver chatted away at first trying to start a conversation but soon gave up. Frank was too tired even to talk. At the hotel he paid the fare with far too much money but walked to reception without waiting for any change.

"Thank you!" shouted the driver behind him and then under his breath, "you chatty bastard."

Frank checked in and paid cash for the one night he planned to spend there. He waited impatiently as the receptionist tapped away on her computer and explained the usual housekeeping and safety points. When she had finally finished Frank grabbed the key from her hand and headed for the room. Once there and inside he collapsed on the bed and fell asleep almost immediately.

He had not felt this tired since he was in the army and even then it had taken days of intensive exercise in the field to make him feel like this. Now a full day awake was enough. He would have brooded about it angrily but the need to sleep was too strong.

In the morning he awoke and it took him a while to come to terms with both his surroundings and his predicament. As the truth of the situation dawned on him one piece at a time, his heart sank. He had slept well but still felt exhausted and unwell. His dreams had been troubled and vivid. Faces laughing at him while he lay helpless. Even in the dreams he was physically weak and unable to move properly.

Now that he was awake he felt little better. This body was flabby, slow and dying. His hope of getting the whole process reversed was unrealistic. Even if he got everyone back to Nebus at gun point and started the process in train, he would be unconscious at some point and therefore completely vulnerable. He had thought he might get Paddy to help and watch his back but how could he convince him of what had happened. No, he was stuck in this dying body. His only realistic option was revenge. Revenge on all of those responsible for screwing up his life and stealing his healthy body. That meant Dr Bobby Bartleman, Dan Bartleman and McCoard. With a bit of luck Claude would get in the way too. If he took them all out he could at least die avenged. Chances were he would be dead before any subsequent trial could take place.

With his decision made he headed for breakfast and found that he had a good appetite. He ordered a full fry up, having reasoned that that wouldn't be what killed him now and helped himself to cereal and orange juice for old times' sake while he waited for the hot food to arrive.

His mood had changed now and he was no longer depressed. Instead he felt the same resolve he had known in his younger days on operations and even way back doing P Company with the Parachute Regiment as a recruit. He had a plan. He had a mission and he was going to see it through whatever. At the end of it he would take his chances. God knows what the police would make of it but that was their problem not his.

"Mad American business man guns down colleagues and British veteran." He almost laughed as he thought of the possible headlines.

Breakfast arrived and the condemned man ate it heartily.

Afterwards on the spur of the moment he rebooked his room for that night. It seemed to make sense to have somewhere to leave his things, such as they were and if by any chance he couldn't track any of the Americans down he would need somewhere to regroup and think through his next move. He showered in his room disgusted at the corpulent body he was trapped in. The experience didn't improve his mood any. Then he realised he had to put the same clothes back on again. The underwear he had brought from the flat would have stopped his circulation if he had tried to wear it. The socks fitted so at least that was something but he hated not having fresh clothes after a shower. He was going to make someone pay for this.

After he had dressed he headed to reception and organised a taxi. Rather than take it all the way to Glasgow he had decided to take a train and buy himself some thinking time without some cheery cabby asking him inane questions all the way. The taxi took him straight to the station where he had been dropped off the night before. He bought a return ticket for Glasgow Central hoping that he would only need it one way and bought a copy of Men's Fitness. The irony of that purchase did not escape him. He knew he looked overweight and he was already feeling tired from the exertion of his basic morning so far. He climbed into the train with some effort and took a seat beside the window, checking that his gun was still safely in the pocket of his tweed jacket.

The magazine remained unread on the journey to Glasgow and instead he looked out of the window at all the familiar places the train passed along the way. He couldn't help a feeling that he was seeing them all for the last time. There was finality to this journey. He started thinking to himself, "Farewell Prestwick, farewell Troon, Barrasie..." He had to admit it was difficult to believe he would ever miss Johnstone, but you never know.

By the time the train arrived in Glasgow central he was sufficiently recovered to have a coffee in the main station. He watched the people rush past towards or from trains and wondered what they were all rushing for. He had to admit rushing was beyond him now but he wanted to savour every part of this moment. Time seemed to have become more precious now that his was running out. He wouldn't rush today if he could avoid it. It might be his last day on earth for all he knew. He wanted it to be as full a day as possible.

He knew from the conversation with Jim that that night at least one of the Bartleman family would be staying at The Crowne Plazza Hotel on the side of the river Clyde opposite the new BBC headquarters. There was no point getting there too early. No, he would have a wander round Glasgow city centre for old times' sake.

He exited the station onto Gordon Street and walked slowly to Buchanan Street. The area had been tarted up since his days as a kid being dragged around by his parents. It had even improved since he had the occasional wild night out here in his teens before joining the army. Somehow he had always liked Buchanan Street. It had changed a lot. It was now paved and fully pedestrianised. All the banks seemed to have shut and reopened as restaurants or pubs. He turned down towards Argyle Street and stopped when he reached the House of Fraser. This shop had always fascinated him as a child. It seemed you could buy anything there. He passed through the first door he came to and wandered about aimlessly through the different departments.

In the men's department a harassed young woman came up to him and asked: "Are you American?"

He stared at her for a second unsure what and whether to answer.

"It doesn't really matter. You look like an American. Can I ask you a favour?"

Without waiting for an answer she led Frank over to a rail of men's tweed jackets.

"Which one would you chose?"

Frank looked at the seriously expensive jackets and suspected he wouldn't choose any of them but the girl was very pretty and he was distracted by that as usual.

He opened his mouth to speak but before he could she said, "Bingo!" and picked up one almost identical to the one he was wearing. "If it suits you it'll suit him." With that she was off to the till to pay for it.

Frank chuckled and continued his trip down memory lane. Frasers always went to town with their Christmas decorations and as a childhood treat he would be brought here to see them. It was just the tail end of summer so they were nowhere to be seen but he could picture them clearly. No sign of Santa either which formed part of the annual outing. Still, even if Santa had been there he couldn't have made Frank's current wish come true.

After a full tour of the building he headed outside to Buchanan Street again. Feeling a little bit hungry he headed for Sloan's, one of his old haunts as a young man. He was tired and felt it but he was also very hungry. He ordered a lunch of steak pie with veg and chips and bought a pint of "heavy" to wash it down with. He looked around at all the business people in their smart suits and the shoppers and felt surprisingly calm. Despite everything that had happened to him over the last two days he was not his usual raging self. He had been able to rationalise his situation and decide on a way forward. Have a plan and stick to it he found himself thinking. Having done so he was now calmly killing time until the person or persons booked into the Crowne Plazza were most likely to be there. He had decided to wait till about half past six or so and then go to the hotel and try and discover which room they were in. Beyond that he would have to play it by ear but with a gun in his hand to focus their minds.

After lunch he had another few beers to use up more time. After five and some whiskies, he decided it would be a good idea to phone Paddy and tell him how grateful he was for everything he had done to help over the years. It was a rambling conversation during which Frank drunkenly cursed the bastards from Nebus for screwing him about but didn't go into any further detail.

Paddy was having a bad day at work before the call and wasn't in any mood for a drunken Frank. It took him a moment to recognise the person at the end of the phone who seemed to have a strangely mixed up accent but when he did and after he had confirmed that Frank was finished in Edinburgh and was drunk as a skunk in Glasgow he terminated the call with two words.

Frank would have felt hurt if he had been thinking more clearly. As it was, he smiled and thought to himself, "good old Paddy."

Chapter Twenty Four

The next time Frank looked at the clock in the pub he realised it was well after six. He checked the gun in his suit pocket and went outside to Argyle Street and flagged down a taxi.

"Crowne Plazza," he slurred and slumped into the back seat.

The driver thought he heard an American accent in there somewhere and hoped for a generous tip. He headed off towards the riverside, following signs for the SECC. He managed to fit in a few extra turns to beef up the fare but soon arrived at the hotel.

In the back of the taxi Frank gathered his thoughts as best he could. He decided the gun would be handier tucked into his waistband and moved it there from the pocket of the tweed jacket while the taxi drove through the thinning rush hour traffic.

"There we are sir," said the taxi driver turning round to face Frank. "That'll be three pounds fifty please."

Frank fumbled for the money in his pocket and as he did so the driver noticed the pistol tucked into his trousers. Taking the twenty pound note he was handed and told to keep all of, the taxi driver thanked his generous passenger without batting an eyelid and waited till he was safely out of the cab. As soon as he was though, the driver got straight on to his central office by radio and got them to inform the police that a passenger in a Tweed jacket had just headed into the Crowne Plazza hotel packing a pistol.

At the reception of the hotel a smartly groomed young Latvian lad looked up and greeted Frank as he arrived.

"Can I help you, sir?" he inquired in perfect English.

"Hopefully," replied Frank. "I'm meeting friends for dinner and wondered if they'd checked in yet. Their name is Bartleman."

The receptionist turned to the screen of his computer and typed some details on the keyboard then waited for the information to come up. When he did he started reading from the screen and then turned to Frank.

Frank had moved round and had leaned over the desk while the man was typing and had just managed to read the number of the room before the receptionist looked up and scowled at him.

"Your friends have arrived. Would you like me to let them know that you are here?"

"No thanks I'm sure they'll be down soon. Just wanted to make sure they had arrived safely."

Frank straightened himself up till he was back in front of the desk but as he did so his jacket flapped open and the receptionist caught a brief glimpse of a gun tucked inside his waistband. Frank wandered off to towards the bar as casually as he could. As soon as he was out of earshot the receptionist phoned his duty manager who phoned the police.

Frank looked over towards the lifts and noticed a large, muscular man sitting very close to them watching all the comings and goings in the hotel. He looked over towards Frank who quickly ducked behind a pillar. He looked round and saw a door marked stairs. As quickly and as smoothly as he could he covered the distance from the pillar to the door and pushed his way through. He had no idea if the guard had spotted him. Either way he was committed now and started climbing to the Suites on the 15th floor.

Almost immediately he realised what a mistake this was. Maybe in his own fit body he could have coped with the climb with relative ease but in Blaine's cast-off he was struggling from the outset. By the time he reached the fourth floor he was breathing hard and sweating like a pig. God he hated this body. But he had to keep going. Each flight of stairs took an eternity and made him feel worse than ever. By the tenth floor he had to stop and have a rest.

Recovery was slow but he knew he had to keep going. Digging deep for every drop of determination he could muster he pulled himself to his feet and set off again. Up and up he went but the climb was taking its toll. The sweat was dripping down his back. His breathing was laboured and his heart was pounding inside his chest in a most worrying fashion. At last he reached the 15th floor and collapsed again onto the landing. He gasped for breath and wiped the sweat from his forehead, soaking the sleeve of his jacket as he did so. His shirt was sodden too and drops of liquid ran down his back, to his cords and then down his legs. He prayed it was only water but he was way past caring.

With gritted teeth he hauled his fat carcass to its feet and made for the door. He was too exhausted to think through what might be on the other side and brushed the door open with a struggle. As he entered the corridor on the other side he saw a large figure 40 feet away sitting outside a room. The man was holding his head which appeared to be bandaged.

Claude looked up at the same time as Frank recognised him. An evil grin formed on Claude's face as he rose to his feet and slowly walked towards Frank.

"Well well well, if it isn't my old friend McCoard," he said flexing the muscles on his neck and arms ready to swing. "I was hoping we might meet again and now my luck is in."

He felt less lucky and stopped smiling when Frank drew the pistol from his belt and pointed it straight at Claude's chest.

"Open the door and let's see who we have inside," said Frank. "No heroics please. I've had a shitty couple of days and would really like to take it out on someone. You'd be perfect."

Reluctantly Claude turned and slowly walked back to the door of Dan's suite. He opened it slowly and was about to rush in and slam the door shut again but felt the gun in the back of his neck. Frank had surprised even himself with how quickly he had moved there after the stairs.

"No tricks now Claude. This is a bit more dangerous than a toilet roll holder and that must have hurt you enough at the time."

Claude moved slowly through the doorway with Frank shadowing his every step. Inside Frank was relieved to see both Bartlemans in the lounge area. He motioned Claude to lead the way. As they entered the lounge Frank stopped dead in his tracks. Standing beside the window was his old self with a glass of whisky in his hand.

The three Americans in the lounge stopped too and looked in amazement at what they recognised as Blaine's body carrying a gun.

"You bastards," Frank shouted at them. "You absolute bastards. Who gave you the right to do this to me?"

Claude was standing with his back to Frank and thought this outburst afforded an opportunity to redeem himself. He spun round and launched himself at Frank, reaching for the gun as he did so. But he had made his last error in what had been a bad, final 48 hours.

Frank turned the gun slightly and fired an unaimed shot at Claude. It hit him in the stomach and only slowed him slightly. Frank took a quick step back and fired a second shot aimed this time directly at Claude's heart. The big American crumpled and lay dead on the floor.

Frank turned to the other three who had all turned quite pale. Only Dan seemed to have retained any form of composure.

"Let's not get carried away here. I'm sure we can work something out. Name your price," he said.

Frank stared at him in disbelief. Blaine was also starring at Dan in disbelief.

"He didn't know, did he?" Blaine said. "You lied to us both."

Frank started to look at his old body as it spoke and suddenly realised they had both been duped.

He looked back at Dan and at his nephew Bobby who was the whitest of them all and looked as if he might throw up. He had obviously been aware of the deception too. Frank was still sweating profusely and his heart had not slowed down since his efforts on the stairs. He felt faint but was determined to see this through to the end.

"I want you to reverse the process. I want to get my body back. Today! Can you do that?" he shouted.

Frank's question was directed at Bobby but it was Dan who answered.

"I'm afraid not Frank. You see we scrubbed the recordings after the process was finished. They take up such a lot of computer space that it would have delayed other projects if we hadn't. We didn't expect to need them again. So it really would be better to negotiate a figure. We can be ridiculously generous with our compensation, all things considered."

"Scrubbed," Frank thought to himself. They had just scrubbed every detail of his personality. There was no way back. Even if he frog marched them back to Edinburgh they would have to start the whole process from scratch. There was no way he could make them do that at gun point. Even if he could persuade Paddy to help, which was very doubtful, the ball would be in their court. They could sabotage his return at any time and nobody else would know. The bastards.

A strange smile spread over his face. If they couldn't undo what they had done he sure as hell could make them pay for it. Yes he was going to die soon but he would make sure they died sooner. The Bartlemans at least. This

McCoard guy had some explaining to do but it looked as if he'd been suckered too, albeit with a better outcome for him.

Frank walked towards Dan and Bobby with the gun pointing straight at Dan's face. Frank could still feel sweat running down his back and his forehead. He felt ill as never before and dizzy but he fought it. He wanted to see a look of fear in these bastards faces before he shot them. He stared at Dan.

"I'm going to shoot you now," he said. His dizziness made it sound detached and added to the menace of the threat.

Dan was about to enter into further negotiations when Frank pulled the trigger. A loud bang marked the passing of Nebus Holding's main shareholder. Dan slumped to a kneeling position and then slowly sank sideways to the floor.

"What are you going to do?" asked Bobby.

"That is the most stupid question I have ever been asked," said Frank. "I thought you were supposed to be really clever."

He pulled the trigger again and this time Bobby shot backwards and hit the floor head first. Frank found himself losing focus. He could no longer keep himself conscious. He looked at his old body standing at the other end of the room. Maybe this Blaine character could sort something out. Either way Frank knew he was no longer able to fight the nausea and dizziness and he passed out on the carpet at the front of one of the two large sofas in the lounge area of the suite. The gun slipped from his hand onto the floor beside him. Instinctively Blaine walked over and picked it up. He wasn't sure exactly why but he didn't want to give Frank a chance of getting hold of it again. Blaine stood there shocked and stunned with the gun in his hand.

Chapter Twenty Five

Scott McDougall had been a policeman for nine years now. He had risen to the rank of sergeant quickly and was respected by his colleagues. He liked being a policeman. He liked being a sergeant. But most of all he liked being part of an armed response team. Carrying guns and knowing how to use them was about as good as it got. He was a great shot. If they had them, he could have shot the whiskers off a fly from fifty feet. The only drawback was that, as yet, he had not had the chance to shoot someone. He had been called out many a time and discovered kids with toy guns, people carrying suspicious parcels and on two wonderful occasions drug dealers with the real thing. Unfortunately they had dropped their weapons when ordered to do so and so, as yet, Scott had not fired a shot in anger.

The call that came in that evening however, sounded more promising. A big guy in a Tweed jacket had been hiding a gun down his cords. Not just one over-imaginative member of the public had called it in but two sober and reliable sources. A cabby who had seen guns before in his taxi, had phoned first. Then a science graduate from Latvia working in a hotel had confirmed the details. Scott had scrambled with his team to the Crowne Plaza and got some brief details from both witnesses. As they did so they heard a muffled gunshot from above and a guest on the 15th floor phoned down to say she had heard gunfire.

Now Scott found himself with half his team at the top of the stairs. The other half were covering the lift and exits. It had been a long hard slog but he and his team were fit and fueled on adrenalin. This was it. This was the real McCoy. Gunfire from a room and no negotiators here yet. One more shot and he could smash through the door and shoot whoever was doing the shooting. The guest's report suggested it had all happened in a suite towards the middle of the corridor he was now staring at. Half way along there was a chair out in the corridor and the door beside it was slightly open. It had swung shut behind someone but not all the way. That looked the most likely location for the gunman.

Scott motioned silently for his colleague Brian Cameron to follow him towards the suite and for the other two members of the team to stay at the stair door in case he was heading for the wrong set of rooms.

Brian was a constable with 12 years' service who had been authorised to carry firearms for eight. He too had never fired a shot in anger and he too thought tonight might just be the chance to change all that. The two men edged towards the door. They knew the gunman was about six foot one and was wearing a Tweed jacket and brown cords. He had a strange accent which was half

Scottish half American and by the sound of it he might even be holding a smoking gun.

Just before they reached the door they heard a gunshot coming from the suite. "Bingo," Scott thought to himself. They couldn't wait for any university trained negotiator now. This was a live situation probably with dead bodies and that put him in charge. He motioned for the other two members of his team to catch up with him and signaled for them to cover himself and Brian.

A second shot rang out and he turned to Brian. They stared at each other and nodded. Scott rushed through the door first and pointed his gun to the right while Brian rushed through just behind him aiming to the left. Nothing and nobody. They moved silently towards the bathroom door and did the same again. Nothing and nobody. Moving quickly they made for the lounge area attached to the suite and took in a scene of carnage.

Where the rooms connected lay a huge bruiser of a man with a bandage on his head. He was lying in a large pool of his own blood and was clearly dead from the angle of his neck. On the floor of the lounge lay two men, one elderly the other a generation younger, but both equally dead from single bullet wounds in the head. A pair of legs in brown cords protruded from the end of a sofa suggesting a fourth corpse hidden there. At the far end of the room, however, near to the windows, stood a tall man in a Tweed jacket and brown cords. A hard looking bastard, Scott thought. The tall man was holding a gun which still had smoke coming out of the barrel and was staring at the gun with a look of confusion on his face. As the two policemen entered the room and leveled their rifles at him he turned and looked at them.

"Drop it!" shouted Scott.

The tall man continued to turn and the gun turned with him.

Scott and Brian both loosed off two shots in quick succession and the man rocketed backwards in a shower of blood. As he did so his face still had the same look of utter confusion on it.

The policemen moved swiftly forward and checked the gunman was dead. They looked round and, seeing no blood on the body beside the sofa, checked it for a pulse. To their surprise they found one and Scott called for the rest of his team to secure the crime scene while he radioed for an ambulance. The paramedics had been called out as part of the standard procedure when the armed response unit was mobilised so they were waiting on the ground floor with the other half of Scott's team.

As the paramedics attended to the only survivor of the slaughter which had taken place, Scott noticed a strange thing. The man they had found lying and still breathing beside the sofa was also wearing a Tweed jacket and brown cords. A quick inspection showed powder marks on his hands from the recent firing of a handgun.

"Shit," thought Scott to himself. "That's a detail we don't want to go public." He turned to the paramedics and asked them to get the casualty to the hospital quickly as he was the only witness. Whether it made any difference or not they soon had Frank on the stretcher and had rushed him off to A&E before the Police investigations team arrived to check out what had happened.

Their investigation was as thorough as ever and concluded that one Frank Chisholm, former soldier and reformed alcoholic, had resumed his old habits and consumed a large quantity of alcohol. Specifically four times the legal limit for driving. A fact corroborated by another former soldier and ex-colleague who had received a rambling phone call earlier in the day. Deciding to redress some grievance with the staff of an American bioscience company for which he had recently been working, he arrived at the Crowne Plaza hotel carrying an illegal firearm believed to have been smuggled back from one of his tours in the Middle East whilst serving with The Parachute Regiment. On arrival at the suite occupied by the Americans and a member of their security staff who he had previously assaulted, he had proceeded to shoot three of them whilst still under the influence of drink. The sole survivor of the rampage, American business man Blaine McCoard, appeared to have fainted during the attack and was therefore not in the assailants line of fire before he was challenged and then shot by the armed response unit. This unit had been mobilised from Pitt Street after the gunman had been spotted by two members of the public who were to be commended for their alertness and prompt response in reporting their suspicions. The armed response unit themselves had followed all procedures correctly and, showing no concern for their own safety had entered the hotel suite after hearing further shots and shot the gunman after giving him a chance to surrender with a correctly delivered challenge. For their bravery and professionalism both Sergeant Scott McDougall and Constable Brian Cameron were to be put forward for consideration of award of the Police Medal. The survivor recovered consciousness but due to underlying health problems was unable to give any detailed statement before being rushed to the USA for specialist medical treatment.

Chapter Twenty Six

Frank Chisholm's funeral was a strange affair to say the least. Press from both sides of the Atlantic had camped outside the crematorium for days before in order to get the best angles. A large police presence had helped keep things in order till the funeral started then reporters had started scrambling and squabbling for space with microphones and handbags becoming lethal weapons in the fight for ratings.

As ever, the organisation of the funeral had fallen to Paddy Dickman. He had spread the word round Frank's old contempories in The Parachute Regiment and placed adverts in the local papers for his fitness clientele. A more challenging task was keeping Frank's ex-wives apart. His first wife had signed a deal with a tabloid newspaper and arrived in a car they had provided flanked by minders. His second wife hadn't thought of that in time and eyed daggers at the first wife throughout. His third wide seemed genuinely upset. So much so, that the newspaper offered her a deal too outside the crematorium which she readily accepted, "for the sake of Frank's children".

Paddy managed to sit them far enough apart in the chapel to avoid an outright fight and placed suitable Paras in between them just in case.

All in all there was a good turnout. As well as the wives and the bewildered children there were 20 or so ex-soldiers and about 30 of Frank's clients who seemed to have genuinely liked him. A former commanding officer turned up to show his respects for a soldier who had saved his life, by all accounts, at the Divis flats during the troubles. There were two people who claimed he had saved their lives when they were suicidal, a smattering of staff from the local authority and some ex-girlfriends. Chief amongst these was a very attractive lady Paddy had never seen before. She introduced herself as Charlotte who had travelled all the way from Carshalton in London for dear old Frank.

"Frank and I go way back," she whispered into Paddy's ear as she arrived at the door of the Chapel.

"Well I never," thought Paddy. "He was a dark horse right enough."

The padre from the Parachute Regiment officiated and kept things light and positive as padres do. He majored on Frank's strengths as a soldier, a boxer and someone who had had a positive influence on many lives both in the forces and in the world of health and fitness. While no saint Frank had battled a lifelong addiction to alcohol with some success. Tragically he had lost this battle and had taken with him the lives of three innocent men. God was called upon to be as lenient as possible and it was over to Paddy to say a few words.

Paddy was used to standing in front of large crowds and speaking, but this took some doing. He relied heavily on his speeches as Frank's best man to put a positive spin on his dead friend. Frank had many redeeming qualities, most well hidden. He had indeed saved lives for sure. He had made unfit people fit. Ultimately though, he had succumbed to his weakness for drink. In a recently rare moment of drunkenness he had taken innocent life. In the end though, he had gone out in a blaze of glory as he had always wished.

Chapter Twenty Seven

Frank slowly became aware that he was lying in a hospital bed. He looked up at the ceiling and failed to recognise any of it. He turned his head with difficulty and noticed two gentlemen in very expensive suits sitting beside his bed.

They looked at each other once they realised he was conscious and the older one spoke slowly.

"I represent the interests of the major shareholders of Nebus Holdings Inc," he began. "I have been made aware of the rather unusual circumstances by which you find yourself here in Omaha. Indeed the rather unusual circumstances by which you find yourself in your present... physical form. It has to be stressed that none of the current major shareholders were aware or a party to any of the activities of their late relatives Daniel Bartleman or Doctor Robert Bartleman and as such accept no liability for their actions."

He paused to check that Frank was listening and understood. Frank managed a brief nod but even that hurt like hell.

Emboldened the lawyer went on.

"I have been authorised to offer you a settlement; a rather generous settlement, in return for your agreement not to take legal action against the corporation or current management of Nebus holdings. As part of that agreement Nebus has withdrawn from the areas of research which have led to this current situation. I have to also stress that this offer in no way suggests liability on our part. Should you reject it and choose to pursue redress through the courts we would vigorously deny your version of events. Let me be candid with you, Mr Chisholm, if I may call you that. Here in America the law is whatever you can afford it to be and we have very deep pockets."

Frank made no movement which the lawyer took to be an agreement of sorts.

"I have been authorised to offer you the following terms. In return for your..."

"Silence," the younger man finished the sentence impatiently.

"Confidentiality agreement," the lawyer corrected, "you will receive a salary of $500,000 index linked for life. The mortgage on your house, currently standing at $789,456 will be redeemed by the corporation giving you full and unencumbered ownership. In addition all share options will be honoured giving you a potential profit at yesterday's closing prices of $1.4 million. As an additional incentive we are prepared to make a one-off payment of $5 million to you as full and final severance payment as you withdraw from the employment of Nebus due to health considerations. I do not expect an answer at this moment but the offer will stand for 48 hours only, to give you time to think it over. I advise you to take it and enjoy life."

The two men stood up as if they had rehearsed it and left the room. Frank drifted into unconsciousness again. He dreamed of Steak-pie and chips, of parachute jumps and of Charlotte of Carshalton.

When he woke again a doctor was sitting next to the bed.

"Hello. How are you feeling?" the doctor asked before quickly adding, "don't try and speak yet, the surgery on your throat is too recent. It will be some time before you can speak properly again. For now a thumbs up will do."

Frank gave a weary thumbs up, completely unaware of what was happening.

The doctor continued. "The surgery to remove the tumors from both your back and your throat have been very successful. It is too early to say with any certainty but we are hopeful that you will make a full recovery in due course."

Frank had no idea now what the doctor was talking about but gave another thumbs up to humour him. It was at that moment that he realised the young man who had accompanied the lawyer, had returned and was again sitting beside his bed.

The young man nodded to the doctor who got up and left the room giving Frank a smile as he went.

"Okay Frank, let's talk turkey here. I'm Josh Bing and I've been brought in to run Nebus holdings. I've dug into what happened under the previous management and ownership and I have to say it ain't pretty. You were sold a dummy by Daniel and Robert Bartleman who set you up to take over Blaine McCoard's aging hulk. But they shafted him too. Yes he had cancer but it wasn't as bad as they told him. Dan got some of his intelligence contacts to alter the results of his tests before they went back to the corporation doctor, Zelnik. Blaine thought he was dying and they sold him a story about some ex-airborne dude with money problems who believed he could beat the cancer with exercise and diet; enter one Frank Chisholm. Truth was, Blaine was a dry run for old Daniel to take over some younger smucks body and live forever, or at least longer than the normal span.

"All goes well with the switch but you get wise to it and do a runner. The scene at the hotel in Glasgow, England, was carnage but there are no further enquiries being carried out. Therefore, we are where we are. You are alive and likely to make a full recovery in Blaine's body. Blaine died in your body and you got the blame of that. There's nothing we can do there. I believe your pal Paddy gave you a lovely send off. The Blaine McCoard we need is effectively dead and therefore cannot run the company. Enter yours truly.

"Daniel and Robert Bartleman are also dead and their considerable holdings in Nebus fall to a total of 13 named members of the extended Bartleman family who cannot believe their luck. My job is to ensure an orderly closure of the previous management's activities and a smooth transition to the new owners desire which is bucket loads of dividends and no hassle. I can do that but I need to know that you are safely out of the picture with no intention of rocking the corporate boat."

He stared at Frank who stared back. After a moment Frank gave him the thumbs up signal. Why not, this had to be a dream or a nightmare.

Josh smiled: "I knew you'd see sense. Things ain't looking too bad for you anyway. I'll be back tomorrow with Cohen the lawyer and you can sign the paperwork, one copy in each name for safety's sake. Till then take it easy."

Josh Bing stood up and left the room. Frank lay there vaguely wondering what was next. He tried to think through everything that had happened but couldn't fight the fatigue and drifted off to sleep. This time his dreams were troubled. Rooms with bloody corpses all covered in bandages like the Mummy returning with its extended family. Drunken fights, bizarre taxi drivers and Americans everywhere.

When he next regained consciousness he could see a pretty blond woman of perhaps 40 sat next to him. When she noticed he was awake she put her finger to her lips.

"Don't try and talk honey," Beth said. "Your throats gonna be sore for a while yet. I'll talk and you just listen. Josh told me they're going to pay you off on health grounds but it sounds like we'll be fine financially. I want you to see it as a chance to spend more time at home with me and the kids."

Frank stared at the woman holding his hand and decided spending time with her might not be too bad an option. She must have been stunning in her 20s because she was a beauty still in her 40s. He smiled at her out of habit and she smiled back and leaned down to kiss him.

"Kids, kids, daddy's awake now."

At the edge of his vision two children appeared and each gave him a kiss on his cheek in turn. They placed cards and flowers on his chest and smiled down at him.

"Clara has joined the drama club at school and Daniel is aiming for the soccer team. Now you'll be at home all the time you can train him for the team."

Frank looked at the kids as they looked down at him. Looked like he was going to have time at last to spend with kids. Not his kids admittedly, but they didn't know that. He even had a kid of his own called Daniel to play football with. More importantly he would have enough money to live comfortably for the rest of his life which was also looking a longer proposition than it had before. Maybe things weren't looking so bad after all. In time he could get this old body back into some kind of shape. The challenge of that he could actually enjoy.

At that point the doctor reappeared and insisted that the family left to allow Frank to rest. Beth insisted the children kissed him again then sent them out to the corridor. Once they were safely outside she kissed Frank full on the lips. Her hand slipped under the covers and caressed his crotch.

"Hurry home honey. I'll be waiting for you," she whispered before kissing him again, giving him a filthy wink and leaving the room.

Frank lay there trying to take everything in. As far as everyone was concerned Frank Chisholm was dead. He was Blaine McCoard to most people here in the states and those who knew otherwise wanted to go along with that viewpoint. On offer was a barrel load of money, the attentions of this sexy wife and the love and affection of two adorable kids. He struggled to come up with a downside to all this after what he had recently faced. He drifted off again and had happy dreams of playing football with two young boys, both called Daniel, barbecues in a backyard somewhere and children performing Shakespeare.

When he next came to he looked up into the eyes of the America beauty from the Nebus canteen in Scotland. Now he knew he was dreaming.

"Don't try and talk Blaine, just listen to what I have to say. I know that you were tricked into thinking you would die of cancer and I know that affected your judgment. I love you but I could never be the cause of breaking up what you have with Beth and the kids. I could never forgive myself for that. But whatever happens I want you to know that I'll be there for you. Even if it is only a stolen moment together once a month or once a year I'll be there waiting for you. That's all I can hope for and it's more than I deserve."

He smiled and gave her a thumbs up which seemed to cover everything here. She smiled and wiped a tear from her eye. Then she put her finger to his lips as he tried to speak, then bent down and kissed him passionately full on the lips. Again he felt a hand stroke his crotch. Then she smiled and left the room.

Frank lay there stunned slowly taking everything in. He was no longer destined to die. He had woken up with money for life, a beautiful wife and kids, a house bought and paid for and now the most beautiful woman in the world, waiting patiently for his phone call to arrange a passionate get together whenever he felt like it .

Oh yes. Many things had changed over the last few weeks but one thing held true. Big Frank "the tank" Chisholm was still on a roll.

Made in the USA
Charleston, SC
03 December 2013